DILBY R. DIXON'S
The Dilbonary

Tony J. Perri

For more information regarding permission, write to:
Vertical Turtle Publishing, LLC. 145 E. University, Suite 5. Mesa, AZ 85201

ISBN: 978-1-54390-610-3
eBook ISBN: 978-1-54390-611-0

Printed in the USA
First Printing 2017

For my beautiful girls, M and M.
I love you to the smooneys and back.

DILOSSARY

BITPOG - \ bit-pog \ : a party

BUMBERNELL - \ buhm-ber-neyl \ : robe

COUPENSENTS - \ koo-pen-sents \ : candy

DILBONARY - \ dil-bon-air-ee \ : a secret journal

FAIREBLOSSOM - \ fair-blos-uh m \ : queen

FURWATTNIDS - \ fur-wot-nids \ : animals

GIDLADER - \ gid-lad-er \ : a dreamer

HUDDLEMUGGER - \ huhd-l-muhg-er \ : king

JINBONE - \ jin-bohn \ : a bully

KWEEK - \ kwee-k \ : crazy

LEMBOT - \ lem-bot \ : snack

NOOK NOOKS - \ noo k-noo ks \ : friends

MACAMOO - \ mak-ey-moo \ : clean

PALLYGO - \ pal-ee-gohl \ : homework

PAWGULL - \ paw-guhl \ : weird

QUIVTAR - \ kwiv-tahr \ : a crown

SMOONEYS - \ smoon-ee s \ : moon and stars

SPINHOOT - \ spin-hoot \ : a sports jock

SWIGGLE - \ swig-guhl \ : a mouthful

VONYS - \ voh-nees \ : potatoes

WIKKE - \ wik-kee \ : a giant

YOUPP - \ yoo-uhp \ : delicious

ZEEM - \ z-eem \ : a plate

TABLE OF CONTENTS

HOW I CAME TO BE

It was late morning on December 21st when my mother, Sandra Dixon, lay restless in a hospital delivery room in the town of Bernard Falls awaiting the birth of me, Dilby R. Dixon, her first and only child.

All night and into that morning, a fluke thunderstorm had come in, one of the worst storms the town had ever seen. The storm had knocked out all the electricity in the area, including the hospitals, as the heavy rains and gusty winds blew through town, wreaking havoc and destruction.

As the rest of the town was safely hunkered down in their homes and shelters, my mother remained nervous and scared squeezing the hand of my worried father, Hyatt Dixon, who stood faithfully by her side.

Flickering emergency lights and flashlights were the only source of light for the doctors and nurses surrounding my mother. The storm was relentless as it raged on with lightning crashing down all around the hospital, creating an electrical storm that rattled and shook the walls.

Apparently, that wasn't enough to stop me from coming into the world, as I arrived in almost complete darkness in the hands of Doctor Biddleman at exactly 11:00 a.m., at which time the storm suddenly stopped.

While my mother cradled me in her arms that morning, everyone in the hospital stopped by her room to see us. They expressed admiration for my mother's bravery, and how lucky of a baby I was to be born without any problems under such conditions. Aside from the devastating storm that took place, I was born six weeks early and yet I was completely healthy.

This was the story of my birth as told to me by my parents when I was old enough to understand. I didn't think much of it back then. It was just an interesting story my parents told me. Now, as I have gotten older, I have discovered that there's much more to this story.

The timing of my birth and the storm were in fact no accident.

CHAPTER 1

I AM WHO I AM

The orange glow of the looming sunset streaked through my bedroom window highlighting the wall that stood just beyond the end of my bed. I raised my hand into the light and closed my fist as though I was capturing a part of the sun. I then opened my hand back up, releasing the energy that had now warmed up my cold hand. I would do this repeatedly until my arm got tired or the sun had disappeared, whichever happened first. I often found myself doing odd things like this to pass the time.

Growing up as an only child in a small town to parents who believed I was their miracle baby certainly limits the things you can do. Having no siblings to talk to or play with, I was forced into finding ways to entertain myself, eventually becoming my own best friend. Like anything else, you adapt and you get accustomed to being a certain way, and my way was solitude. Aside from my parents, I was alone in the world, and I was okay with that.

As a baby, everything seemed to come easily and naturally to me. My parents said that I always slept through the nights and rarely cried, even when I had wet diapers. I took my first steps when I was seven months old, and I spoke and understood words more quickly than expected. I was their special child they would say, but I don't think they realized just how special I really was.

As I continued to get older I started to develop a wild imagination, as I would daydream and make up extraordinary stories and places. My parents would laugh at them and tell me what a creative imagination I had. They eventually started calling me their little dreamer because that's what I was.

When I turned five years old, I started school.

I knew when I started that it wasn't going to be easy for me to fit in and make friends. Ever since I can remember, I lacked confidence in myself. I always shied away from things and people, never daring myself to take those big leaps, to be bold and fearless. I might have been taller than most kids my age, but being tall didn't stop other kids, even smaller ones, from intimidating me. If there ever was a confrontation or an uncomfortable situation, I was always quick to back down or walk away. I hated not being able to stick up for myself, something I was always afraid of doing. I was ignored and made fun of because I was different than most kids. Being that kind of kid and having no friends only pulled me down further into seclusion.

This went on for the next five years, as I remained the loner kid in school. Then something very odd happened on the day of my 10th birthday, something that made me look at myself and really see that not only did I not fit in school, but that I just didn't fit in this world.

There I was, walking on the sidewalk minding my own business outside of Goodwin Elementary School after school just got out. I was on my way home when something on the ground caught my eye. I stopped and looked down to watch hundreds of ants scurry through the cracks in the sidewalk in a single line rushing past one another like they had a purpose. What were all these ants doing? Were they running away from something or toward something unknown?

While looking down and lost in thought of these ants, I failed to notice the rumbling of a car speeding past me or the object that was launched from it that exploded all over me and knocked me to the ground, causing my backpack to fly off.

I remained frozen for a second, confused about what exactly just happened. I didn't know what it was that hit me until I wiped the mush out my eyes. I had been pelted by a flying watermelon.

Laughter and hollering came from the car before it screeched its tires around the corner and disappeared.

I lay there covered from head to toe in red, sticky fruit, as I was clearly the victim of a drive by fruiting. The impact from the watermelon caused a little bit of pain in my left arm and chest, but for the most part I was okay.

Before I got up, I heard laughter coming from behind me by the school. I turned around and saw Riley Rogers and his band of no-gooders, Johnny and Billy, leaning against the school wall, pointing and laughing hysterically at me.

Riley was the school bully and Johnny and Billy were like his puppy dogs, always following him around and doing every-thing Riley said. They were mean kids and always had it out for me ever since the 3rd grade.

One day for no reason, Riley took my dad's old hat I was wearing and wrote "loser" in big black marker across the back.

Then he forced it back on my head and pointed at it calling me a loser in front of everyone to see. Needless to say, I never liked him or the no-gooders since that day. And as much as I loved that hat, I never wore it again.

"Hey Dilby, how's that watermelon taste?" Riley yelled out.

"Yeah, how's it taste?" Billy said.

I looked away and ignored their sarcastic remarks knowing any interaction with them would only make it worse.

I got up from the sidewalk and stood there amidst a sea of red, humiliated and embarrassed as the juice dripped off my head, hitting the sidewalk below where pieces of the fruit lay broken all around me.

"Maybe if you weren't spacing out like you always do you might of saw it flying at ya," Riley said with a chuckle.

"Yeah, ya' space case," Johnny said.

"That thing just clobbered you," Riley said.

"Boom, Dilby goes down," Johnny said.

I continued to pay no attention to them as I brushed all the remaining fruit off my face and body. My clean white t-shirt and jeans were now stained red. I looked like a character out of a horror film.

"Why don't you guys just leave him alone!" a voice yelled out.

I looked up and saw Grace Billings walking over to me. Grace and I knew of each other but by no means were we friends. She was also known as Brace Face Grace because she wore braces on her teeth. A name she no doubt got from none other than Riley Rogers himself.

"Are you okay?" Grace asked.

I was rather shocked to see that Grace had come over to help me and I could see that she was genuinely concerned.

"Yeah, I'm fine," I replied.

"Awe, look at that, Brace Face Grace to the rescue," Riley said. "Ain't that sweet?"

"I think I'm gonna cry," Billy said.

"Don't forget to kiss him where it hurts," Riley said as he puckered his lips and made a kissing noise.

I'm not sure how other kids would have reacted to this, whether they would have cried or gotten angry or ran away, but I calmly stood there next to Grace pretending I didn't hear them as I rubbed my left arm where the watermelon hit me.

"Just ignore them, they're jerks," Grace said.

"That's pretty much what I always do anyway," I said.

"You sure you're okay?" Grace asked.

"I'm fine, really," I said.

Just then, we heard a honk. Grace looked to a car that pulled up in front of the school.

"I gotta go," Grace said.

"Thanks, for coming over," I said.

Grace acknowledged me with a smile then walked away and got in the car.

"Looks like you scared her off," Riley said.

I tried to restrain myself from acknowledging him but I couldn't help it any longer, so I turned and threw Riley a dirty look. I knew it was a mistake when I looked at him. I let him get to me and I hated that.

Riley and the no-gooders pushed off from the wall and made their way to me. Riley was out front with Johnny and Billy a few steps behind, one on each side of him.

I looked away and bent down to retrieve my backpack as I knew it was time to get out of there. But before I stood up, Riley grabbed a piece of the watermelon from the ground and slapped it on my head and started rubbing it in.

"I think they missed a spot," Riley said laughing.

"Now, you're a redhead," Billy said. "Get it? Redhead, cause the watermelon…"

"Yeah, we get it, stupid," Riley said looking to Billy.

Riley let the piece go as it slid off my head and fell to the ground. I stood back up with my backpack in my hand and slung it over my shoulder.

"You got something you want to say?" Riley said.

"Nope," I said.

I wiped the fruit from my head, turned and walked away.

"Later, loser," Riley said.

"Yeah, enjoy your walk home," Billy said.

"Enjoy your walk home?" Riley said to Billy.

"Yeah, cause he's like all sticky and stuff," Billy said.

"Whatever. Come on, let's go," I heard Riley say as they walked off.

When I got home, the juice on my body and hair had dried. My fingers would stick together when I squeezed them long enough and my hair looked like the fur of a dirty rat. When my mother saw me, she shrieked at the sight of me. I was already embarrassed and humiliated enough and that only made it worse.

She asked if I saw who it was or why they would do that in which I responded that I didn't know. She then asked if I was okay and then comforted me for a moment before sending me off to get cleaned up.

I didn't have an answer for this happening except maybe it was a case of being at the wrong place at the wrong time. Or maybe Riley was right. If I didn't space out all the time, maybe I would have seen the watermelon coming. Either way, it happened and there was nothing I could've done to change that. All I could do was move on and hope the jokes from Riley and the no-gooders wouldn't last too long.

My birthday wasn't turning out to be so happy and I wasn't in the mood to celebrate. But my parents insisted on taking me out to dinner, in hopes I would forget about what happened after school. Not even dinner at my favorite restaurant took my mind off the drive by fruiting incident. And my hair still smelled like watermelon juice.

Later that night, as my parents and I drove home from the restaurant, my mind ventured away from the fruit bombing. Out of nowhere, I felt happy inside as I thought about the trip to my Aunt Lacy's house two years earlier.

You see, my birthdays were rather boring and uneventful on account of having no friends to invite. So, ever since I was five years old, I chose not to have a party every year. My birthday celebrations would usually be me, my parents and grandparents going out to a restaurant of my choice and then back home to unwrap my gifts. My parents must have felt really sad for me every year which is probably why they always went out of their way to make me feel special and loved with all the gifts.

It was my 8th birthday when my parents decided to change it up and take me on a road trip to see my Aunt Lacy who lived about seven hours away in another state. Aunt Lacy was my mom's older sister and I usually only saw her every other Christmas and during the summer because she was always traveling for work. But no matter where she was or what she was doing, she always had time to call me and send me a gift on my birthday. So making this extra trip was special to me because she always knew how to make me feel like a normal kid.

My mother used to tell me that Aunt Lacy was the cool sister when they were growing up. She was a free spirited girl who always lived life to its fullest and did what made her happy, no matter what anyone else thought. She never wanted to be tied down to anything or anyone, which is why she never got married, my mother would say.

Aunt Lacy was super nice and funny and always made sure that my time with her was fun and exciting. She had a way about her that made me comfortable enough to be myself around her and I could just be the awkward kid that I was and she accepted me for that. She once told me that if people don't like you for who you are, then they weren't meant to be part of your life.

"You know what's so endearing about you, Dilby," she once told me. "That you never try to be someone you're not."

Her words always inspired me to keep true to myself even though I was different than most kids.

Over the years we developed a special bond and every time I visited we would go get ice cream cookie sandwiches and then we would sit in the park and laugh about the stories she would tell me about her and my mom growing up. This became our thing we did and I loved every second of it.

So on the weekend of my 8th birthday when we arrived at Aunt Lacy's, everything was just as I remembered. She greeted me with a big, warm hug and said how much she missed me.

Later, we went to get our treat and talked and laughed in the park as we always did. My life may have been small and boring but with her it felt big and adventurous.

That night, for my birthday dinner, we went out to this Moroccan restaurant that Aunt Lacy told me about where you eat with only your hands. No forks, no knives, just your fingers and the food. Typically, that wouldn't be a place I'd pick, but the whole experience of eating with just your fingers sounded like a good time.

At first, my parents didn't like the idea of eating without silverware, but when they saw how much fun Aunt Lacy and I were having, they soon found themselves diving in and enjoying it. Food was everywhere on the table. Sauce all over our faces, rice stuck in our hair, our hands gooey and sticky. But we didn't care. That was kind of the point, to be messy. At least that's what I thought.

Now, the food may have not been the best for my taste, but it was without a doubt the most fun birthday dinner I'd ever had! Aunt Lacy always knew how to have a good time.

After dinner we went back to Aunt Lacy's to open up gifts. My parents got me stuff that they thought I needed like some clothes and a backpack along with some things they thought I wanted like craft stuff, a skateboard, a scooter, and some money. They were all great gifts but a skateboard and scooter didn't really suit me. I never once wanted or asked for either one of them in my life. I'm not sure but I guess they were trying to give me what other kids had in hopes that maybe I would be like the other kids. Needless to say, I only used them one time so they would think I liked them.

Now, as far as Aunt Lacy's gifts go, she always got me things that spoke to me, gifts that I could relate to and appreciate.

Her first gift was a book titled "I Am Me, You Are Us."

It was a book about a social outcast and a lonely bounty hunter set in the near future where the two come together and forge their way into a changing, controlled society.

"It might be a hard read for you and somewhat difficult to understand considering you're only eight years old," Aunt Lacy told me. "But give it a shot. I think you'll like it."

The book definitely got my interest and for the next five weeks I never put the book down. The book was hard to read like she said and rather slow at times and it did have some things that made me wonder. And after completing the book I realized that I was kind of like the main characters, alone and trying to find their place in the world while challenging and overcoming whatever got in their way. I guess that was the point of this gift, to show me that I too can be that way if I wanted.

Her next gift was a telescope.

"So you can see more of what's out there rather than just what's around here," Aunt Lacy said as she pointed to the sky and then to the ground.

I never knew looking up at the sky could be so fascinating. She was a believer that we as humans weren't the only ones that inhabited this world, that there has to be something or some-one else out there. And the more I looked through that tele-scope out into the dark atmosphere; I began to believe that as well.

The third and final gift Aunt Lacy gave me was a gift similar to what someone had once gave to her. It was a small wooden box carved with geometric designs with a lock and an ornate key. It was called a wishwish box and this is how Aunt Lacy told me how to use it.

"First, you make a fist with one of your hands. Then, you think of a wish. When you have it, whisper that wish into your fist by blowing it through the hole between your forefinger and thumb. Once it's in your fist, quickly release it into the box and close the lid where it stays locked away until that wish comes true. When it does, you open the box and let it go back into the world for someone else to have. Then you just repeat the process with another wish in hopes of it coming true."

"That is so cool," I said with excitement.

"There is one rule though that you must never break no matter what," Aunt Lacy said.

"What's that?" I asked.

"You must never tell anyone your wish. If you do, it won't come true," Aunt Lacy said.

"I won't, I promise," I replied.

It might have been just a simple wood box to most, but to me it represented much more than that. The wishwish box was the best gift I had ever received and it helped me hope for a better future.

"Aunt Lacy, has your wish come true yet?" I asked referring to her wishwish box.

"No, it still remains locked but hopefully one day soon I can open it," she said, looking a little wistful. "Wishes do come true. You just have to believe."

Later that night, I went outside and looked up at the night sky as I held onto the wishwish box. I thought about how much I loved coming to Aunt Lacy's and all the great gifts I got and how lucky I was to have such a great family. I was thankful for my parents for bringing me here and for everything they do for me. But neither my parents or Aunt Lacy or anyone else, including myself, could give me what I truly wanted. I needed help from a higher power and so I looked to my wishwish box.

As I sat alone on the splintered wooden steps of my aunt's porch holding onto the wishwish box on my lap, I closed my eyes and thought up a wish. When I knew what I wanted, I then opened the wishwish box, whispered that wish into my fist and then released it inside, quickly closing the top. With a turn of the key my wish was now locked away until the day it would come true. I tied the key to a string and put it around my neck where it would stay until the day comes to use it.

It was two years later since I got the wishwish box and I had yet to open it. It remained resting on my dresser drawer and the key still hung around my neck as a constant reminder to not lose faith, that my wish would come true.

CHAPTER 2

EARTH TO DILBY

We arrived back home from dinner and I had decided to stay out in front of the house for a little while since it wasn't bedtime yet. The air was cool and peaceful and I wanted some time to just be alone.

As I sat on the porch looking up at the sky, my mind went blank. It became so quiet I could almost hear nothing, as though I went deaf and I could feel everything slowing down as though time was stopping. Then, all I could see was black and poof, I was transported to another place and time.

And that was how my daydreams happened every time.

This particular daydream wasn't the first one I had, but it was the first time I had daydreamed of a place that wasn't inspired by watching TV or looking through a book. This dream was purely of my own doing.

In the dream, I was walking across a rocky and jagged mountainside as menacing gray clouds slowly moved above me. As I made my way up the mountain, the clouds shifted lower and soon I found myself walking through them. The density of the thick clouds lessened my visibility as I could only see about 5 feet in front of me.

Then, as if the thick fog wasn't enough to put a little fear into me, I heard a strange voice call out in a language I never heard before. I remained quiet as I quickly looked around but I couldn't see much of anything. The strange voice once again spoke out. Just then, the clouds thinned out in front of me and I could now see a cave not far from where I was.

As I cautiously approached it, I heard the voice again, only this time I could see where it was coming from. I couldn't believe what I was seeing. The voice I had heard was coming from the cave. The cave was actually speaking to me.

The opening of the cave was like a mouth and every time it talked, a rush of air would come out and blow my hair. As it talked, I began to somehow understand and speak its language. It asked me who I was and if I had come to seek answers. I didn't know what it meant by that, but for the next few minutes we exchanged friendly words.

It had invited me to enter into its mouth but I choose not to go in. It told me I would find what I was looking for inside and all I had to do was enter. The adventurous part of me wanted to get swallowed up, but the rational part of me convinced me not to go in. It wasn't the fact that I was scared to go in, okay, well maybe a little, but I was just more fascinated that I was having a conversation with a cave.

And so when I refused to enter, the cave went quiet and slowly disappeared into the thick clouds that rolled back in. All the light had quickly gone away and soon all that remained was blackness.

When I came out of my daydream, my parents were call-ing out to me.

"Hey, where did you go there, big guy?" Father asked.

"You okay, sweetie?" Mother asked as she leaned into me.

"Yeah, I'm fine. Why?" I said.

"We were talking to you for like 10 seconds and you didn't respond." Father said.

"You had us worried," Mother said. "You were just sitting there looking up at the sky."

"I was just thinking about stuff," I said.

"Like what?" Father asked.

"Stuff. I guess I just spaced out," I said. "I'm fine, you don't need to worry."

Mother and Father looked to each other as though there was something to be concerned about. For the time being they let it go as I got up and went inside the house to my bedroom.

As I laid in bed thinking about my daydream, I really didn't give much thought to the odd language the cave spoke or the fact that a cave could speak at all. What I did think about was what was inside that cave. What did I miss out on by not venturing inside?

I could only assume that from all that I had seen and read, that I was now able to create my own places and things from inside my own little mind. This was much different from what I would dream about before. My dreams were never this detailed or vivid like this one. This was something much more. I was scared at first by all this because this was new to me, but then the fear of it all went away and turned into excitement.

My parents and teachers could always tell when I was daydreaming by the blank look that appeared on my face as I would gaze off in the distance, staring out into an empty space. And I would often hold on to the key tied to the string that was around my neck.

"Hello...Dilby...anyone home," my parents would say to me, snapping their fingers until I answered them.

Or teachers would say, "Earth to Dilby. Come back, Dilby," as the other kids laughed.

Sometimes I would get so deep into my daydreams that a voice or even snapping fingers wouldn't bring me back. My parents and teacher would have to bang something together real loud until I responded. This of course drew more concern from my parents to the point they wanted to take me to a doctor. I argued and fought to not go and promised them it was nothing to be worried about.

"This isn't funny anymore, this is serious, Dilby," Mother said.

"I can control them," I said. "I promise I'll be better."

I understood that my daydreaming was becoming a big concern for everyone, but I was a good kid and a good student who got good grades. So what harm was it doing? The fact was I couldn't control it and I didn't want it to stop either.

Daydreaming quickly became my favorite thing to do as it would occur more and more and without me even trying. It would just happen anytime and anywhere that my mind felt the need to escape. It was like my mind had a mind of its own!

When I would awaken from my daydreams, I would remember odd sounding words and their meanings that I heard in my daydreams, such as the word **PAWGULL***. There was something special about these strange new words because they meant something to me. The words made sense to me. It was as though I was making up my own language with all these new words.

It was around that same time that I had really noticed my body and appearance had changed. My body thinned out and I grew like a weed as I was told I was tall for my age. I wore baggy clothes most of the time, usually jeans with holes in them, and almost always had a red colored shirt.

"Why do you only wear red shirts?" kids would occasionally ask. "Why is the sun yellow?" I would respond. I always answered back with some sort of stupid question like that because I just thought it was more interesting than the truth, which was that I just liked red shirts.

My hair was brown, shaggy and almost touched my shoulders. Sometimes I wore a hat, but not my dads old hat. Riley ruined that one for me.

Lastly, I refused to wear anything but my favorite pair of white sneakers with red stripes on them, which I proudly cleaned every night because I wanted them to look like they were new.

So yes, I was different in many ways, but how I looked and dressed is not how I became who I am. My imagination was creating my dreams and I was about to be thrown a curveball that would prove dreams could be just as real as the world we live in.

CHAPTER 3

THE WONDERFUL WORLD OF COUPENSENTS

It was a Thursday afternoon during spring break when I daydreamed of a place made entirely of candy. This daydream, however, wasn't my average, ordinary daydream. This was something much different and I was convinced that maybe these weren't just daydreams anymore.

It was unseasonably hot out that day, too hot for me to be doing something outside so I decided to stay indoors in my cozy, cool bedroom. As I lay on my unmade bed, bored, my eyes floated around the room searching for ideas of something I could do to occupy my time.

My eyes stopped at the dresser where a bag full of candy that I got for doing all my chores sat staring back at me next to the wishwish box.

My parents never really let me have a lot of sugar. In fact, I was only allowed to have candy every once in a while and on special occasions like holidays or birthdays. Candy was a luxury so I didn't miss it all that much when I didn't have it. But when I had it, I wanted a lot of it.

"Too much candy will rot your teeth away and give you a bellyache," I remembered my parents always telling me.

Was this really true? Or was it something they just said to scare me into not eating a lot of candy? Maybe it was a little bit of both.

I knew it was only 10 o'clock in the morning, but any time is a good time for candy, right?

I jumped up from the bed, grabbed the bag, and plopped down on the floor. I dumped all the candy on the carpet and began to separate them into piles, just to see what I had. There were suckers, sour gummy worms and bears, taffy, chocolate malt balls, chocolate raisins, and some assorted gumballs. The sweet smell of sour, gummy, chocolate heaven was making me **KWEEK*** and I wanted to eat it all, but I knew I couldn't. However, a few pieces of each type of candy never hurt anyone, so in my mouth they went.

After I had finished sorting my candy into piles and having a few more chocolate balls, I laid down in between the piles with my head resting on the gummies. I thought about what would really happen if I suddenly just ate all of it right then and there. Would I really get a bellyache like my parents always said? Would my teeth really rot away?

As I lay there staring at the piles, it became quiet and everything slowed down.

Then, all I could see was black and I was off in a daydream.

As I entered my daydream, I remembered sitting up, my eyes filled with wonder and amazement as I looked out onto an unfamiliar place. As far as I could tell, everything in that place was made out of candy!

I quickly stood up and made my way through that luscious land, taking it all in. It was incredible and glorious and it was all real.

There I was, standing in a place made entirely of candy and as far as I could see, I was the only one there. There were no parents there to tell me I couldn't eat what I wanted, and no other kids to take it away from me. And so without thinking twice, I began to stuff my face with all of it!

I was like a tornado swallowing up everything in its path as I ran through the marshmallow meadows shoveling gobs of the sticky, white, fluffy treat in my mouth as it oozed out the sides.

Then I came to the chocolate frosted fields, where I rolled around covering my sticky marshmallow body from head to toe, becoming a giant chocolate covered marshmallow, slurping the sweet chocolate from my hands.

From there, I crawled out of the fields and dove into the lemonade lake. I swam through the cool refreshing lemonade as the chocolate marshmallow slithered off my body. It was the best lemonade I had ever tasted and I gulped it down. Gulp, gulp, gulp!

After my stomach had filled with the lemony liquid, I made my way to a red road that wove its way through a lollipop forest.

The red road was soft, squishy, and kind of sticky. I bounced on it a bit before I ripped a piece of it off and tasted it. Holy cow, it was cherry taffy! The road was made out of cherry taffy! Who could have ever imagined a thing like that? That place was so sweet-tacular and there was still so much more to see and taste.

As I continued my journey through that place, I licked and bounced my way down the squishy cherry taffy road, playing with and eating just about everything I could get my hands on along the way.

I bit through the butterscotch bark, ripped into the raspberry filled rocks, grazed on the gummy grass, licked the licorice tree limbs, jumped in the jelly bean bushes, collected the cotton candy clouds, devoured the gumdrop daisies, and popped the peanut butter balloons! I had eaten so much candy that it would surely make any parent freak out, and make any kid the happiest they'd ever been. I truly was in the sweetest place in the world.

As I sat rubbing my belly full of sugar, I looked around and remembered that I was all alone in this place, just me and my sweet tooth. At first, the idea of that sounded perfect. Sure, I had all the candy in the world I could eat, but would candy be enough to make me happy?

"What's wrong Dilby?" I heard a voice say. "Why do you look sad?"

I quickly looked around to see where the voice was coming from, but no one was there. Was all the candy I ate making me hear things?

"Psst, over here, in front of you," the voice said.

Standing in the distance up ahead was a giant, black licorice tree. It was the only tree in the lollipop forest that wasn't a lollipop and it was motioning me to come to it. First there was a talking cave and now a talking licorice tree!

I cautiously made my way over to it.

"That's it, don't be afraid," the licorice tree said.

"You can talk?" I said as I reached the tree and stood in front.

"I sure can and I can move too," the licorice tree said.

Its trunk was it's mouth and the branches were arms that were limp and flailed around when they moved, like a licorice stick does.

"That's amazing," I said.

"Kind of like this place," the licorice tree said. "Could you think of a better place you would want to be in? A land made of **COUPENSENTS*** that you can eat forever."

"Coupensents?" I said. "You mean candy?"

"That's what I said, coupensents," the licorice tree said. "There is everything here you would ever want and more. Just ask and it will be provided to you."

"Anything?" I asked.

"Just name it and it's yours," the licorice tree said.

"Hmm, let me think...how about a candy corn pine cone," I said.

The licorice tree branches began to move, whipping its flimsy arms all around. Then, from atop the licorice tree, I heard something falling. I looked up and spotted a small object bouncing its way down, hitting the licorice arms until it landed on the ground by my feet. I bent down and picked it up. It was a pine cone in candy corn colors!

"Go ahead, eat it," the licorice tree said.

Without a second thought I chomped into it. It felt and tasted just like candy corn and it was delicious.

"Anything else you can think of?" the licorice tree asked.

Sadness suddenly came over me. My interest and desire for coupensents had gone away.

"Thanks, but I don't want anything else," I said, dropping the pine cone on the ground.

"Do you not like it here?" the licorice tree asked.

"No, I think this place is incredible. It's just…" I said with a pause.

"It's just not what you thought it would be?" the licorice tree said.

"There's nothing but coupensents here," I said.

"Well, isn't that what you wanted?" the licorice tree replied. "To have all the coupensents in the world?"

"Yeah, but how much coupensents can a kid eat?" I said.

"Aha, so you're missing something or someone," the licorice tree said.

"The longer I'm here, the more I begin to miss my home," I said. "And I don't think I'd be truly happy if I was somehow stuck here all by myself. I'd miss my parents and they would miss me too. And that makes me sad."

"Well then, Dilby, you should run," the licorice tree said.

"What?" I said.

Suddenly, I heard the faint sound of something pounding in the distance. I looked around to see where the noise was coming from, but saw nothing. I stood silently listening as the sound grew louder and closer. I could hear things breaking, almost like the sound of glass shattering.

Off in the distance, I saw something big and yellow rolling down a hill, crushing every lollipop in its way. As it got closer, I could see it was a giant gumball and it was heading straight toward me, getting bigger and closer with every second.

All I could think to do was run like the licorice tree told me. I took off and ran as fast as I could down cherry taffy road, but the squishiness of the road slowed me down and the giant gumball boulder was gaining on me.

I veered off the road into the lollipop forest but the giant gumball seemed to follow me. No matter where I went, it was right on my tail, as if it wanted to crush me. I screamed and tried to run faster but the candy in my belly seemed to slow me down and I could feel the gallon of lemonade I drank earlier swishing from side to side.

The giant gumball was right behind me and all I could think was that I didn't want to be crushed by this thing. I had enough coupensents and I was ready to return home.

Suddenly, the ground beneath me turned to mush and I sank right in it. The ground was like quicksand and it had sucked me right down as I quickly disappeared from the lollipop forest, barely having escaped being crushed by the giant gumball.

CHAPTER 4

I GOT COTTON CANDY IN MY PANTS

I jolted awake from the daydream as I was gasping for air. My eyes flew open and I found myself lying on my bedroom floor just as I was when I left it. As I lay there catching my breath, I realized that the giant gumball didn't get me after all and I was safe and sound back home. Except, instead of resting my head on a pile of gummies, my head was flat on the empty floor.

Most of the piles were gone and there were a few pieces of coupensents scattered around me. My mouth was coated with chocolate and sugar and there were gummies stuck in my hair. This was bad. This was very bad.

If my parents were to suddenly walk in, I would surely be in one bad, sticky situation.

When I got off the floor, I noticed that my front jean pockets were bulging out, like they were filled with something. Confused and curious, I felt the outside of the pockets. They were soft and spongy and when I pressed on them, they poofed back out. I then slowly reached in both front pockets and surprisingly pulled out handfuls of pink and blue cotton candy.

This was beyond pawgull because I didn't have cotton candy in my jeans or my coupensents bag before I daydreamed of that sweet place. So where could this cotton candy have come from then? Would I… could I… did I somehow magically bring back cotton candy clouds? No way, I must be going kweek? This can't be possible? Could it be possible? I didn't know what to think except maybe I was still dreaming.

There was a knock at the door.

"Dilby, sweetie, you want a snack?" Mother asked.

Oh no, if she were to come in, she would see everything. I'd be busted for sure.

"No thanks, not hungry," I said as I stood up and quickly gathered up the few remaining coupensents and cotton candy clouds and threw them back in my bag.

"Okay then," Mother said as I heard her walk away from the door. I shoved the bag under the bed behind some toys to hide it for now.

Right about then, I felt a sharp pain in my stomach. It was so painful that it dropped me to my knees. I hunched over and quickly wrapped my arms around my stomach, squeezing against it hoping it would somehow take away the pain. This must be the bellyache my parents warned me about when you eat too much coupensents.

I quickly realized that I wasn't still dreaming after all!

As I sat there on the floor clutching my stomach in agony, I couldn't stop thinking about that cotton candy. I didn't think about eating it, but more about if it was actually real or just my imagination. Thinking about the cotton candy actually took my mind off my stomach pain because it started to not hurt as bad.

I grabbed the coupensents bag from under the bed and opened it. I looked inside and there it was. I reached in and took out the cotton candy. I held it in my hands and just stared at it as though it was some priceless jewel.

It felt real. It looked real. It smelled real. I tasted it and yes, it was real.

"How could this be possible?" I thought.

I had no logical explanation for what had happened. None. Not only was I able to travel to a different world in my daydream, but I was able to bring something back.

"This is so awesome!" I said to myself in excitement.

I knew I could dream up anything, but this, this changed everything. The possibilities seemed limited only by my imagination and I had a very big imagination.

My stomach pain came back and it was worse than what it was the first time. I managed to get back up from the ground and walk over to my wall mirror where I stood hunched over staring at myself. I looked like a mess. The gummies were still stuck to my hair, dangling just past my shoulder, and my face was covered in melted chocolate with taffy stuck to it.

As I stared into the mirror, I forced myself to stand upright. I fought through my stomach pain as I felt a surge of power, an energy that shot right through me. I ripped the gummies from my hair and threw them on the ground. I straightened my shirt, fixed my hair, and wiped the chocolate and taffy from my face. I stood up tall and puffed out my chest like I was some superhero.

In that moment, I was no longer just another 10 year old outcast kid that no one liked. I was Dilby R. Dixon, the world's first "time dreamer."

A smile formed on my face as I stood proud of myself. Something in me changed in that moment. I was a somebody now.

I wasn't quite sure of how I came up with the name time dreamer or what it even meant but it was the first thing that popped into my head when I was looking at myself in the mirror. I had never spoke those words or heard them before, but yet for some mysterious reason they sounded and felt familiar to me.

Out of nowhere my stomach started to rumble. I could feel something making its way up from inside my stomach up to my mouth, like a volcano about to erupt. And before I knew it, my proudest moment was over as I vomited all over the mirror in front of me. The vomit was a rainbow of colors, no doubt a mixture of all the different candy I ate and it came out of me like a fire engine hose, covering the whole mirror as it slid its way to the carpet like a chunky technicolor slimeball. I wiped the disgusting ooze from my mouth as I stood there catching my breath.

I wanted something more, something bigger, and that's exactly what I got.

CHAPTER 5

WORDS TO LIVE BY

It was the summer before 6th grade when things really started changing for me. My status on the social ladder at school when 5th grade ended was still on the bottom. In fact, I wasn't even on the ladder at all.

For the most part, that really didn't bother me and I tried not to pay attention to it like I've always done. Besides, I had more important things to think about, such as my daydreams, which I continued to have. Not only was I having them more frequently, but I was remembering the details more and more.

One night during dinner I asked my mother to put some **VONYS*** on my **ZEEM***.

My parents looked at each other like I was kweek, clearly not understanding what I was talking about. At that time, it didn't even occur to me I had said those words. They had rolled off my tongue and out of my mouth so naturally as if they were real words.

"What?" my mother said looking confused.

It wasn't until I had asked again that I realized what I had said the first time.

"The potatoes, can you put some on my plate please."

My mother furrowed her eyebrows as she grabbed my plate and proceeded to put some potatoes on it. She handed the plate back to me and I immediately began to scarf them down, hoping that was the end of it, but it wasn't.

"Did you learn a new language, sweetie?" Mother asked.

"What do you mean?" I said.

"Those words you just said, where did you learn them?" Father asked, chomping on his food.

I paused a moment before answering.

"What words?" I said, trying to play it off.

"The words you just said. It was like zeem and something else?" Father said as he washed down his bite of food with his cold drink.

"Was it from a book or something?" Mother asked.

"Yeah, a book...from the library," I blurted out.

"Well, what's the book called?" Mother asked.

"I don't remember, just some book," I said.

"Well, it sounds weird," Father replied.

"But interesting," Mother said, with a caring smile.

"Uh huh," I said as I continued to stuff my face until my plate was empty.

The words didn't seem to make any sense to my parents, they just thought I was being cute and silly, like how most kids can be. The only thing was that I wasn't like most kids.

My daydreams were happening almost every day now with some shorter than others, but each one more pawgull than the last. More daydreams meant more new words and that was exciting to me.

It took a lot for me to be excited about anything because I really didn't have anything exciting to look forward to. But when I started to make up this new language, it was like my world just suddenly opened up and it was exciting and infectious. The only problem was that I didn't have anyone to share this new language with. I was still fearful about using them around my parents since the first time didn't go so well.

Since the age of seven, my relationship with my parents was kind of distant, much more so with my father than my mother. The older I got, the more pawgull I would become, which in turn caused me to not be very close with my parents. I knew I was different and I didn't think they understood me. At times, I felt like I didn't belong there. I thought my parents looked at me the same way the kids in school did and that they didn't want anything to do with me. But that wasn't the case at all. That was just my mind projecting those feelings because I had gotten used to being ignored by everyone else.

I wasn't into sports or any type of physical activity like my father was, which led to us having nothing in common, which caused us to hardly ever spend time together. Our conversations were always brief and uneventful, on account of us having nothing to talk about that interested both of us.

My mother didn't really get me either, but she constantly made an effort to try to not make me feel like I was an outsider. She always asked me about school and how I was doing and if she could do anything for me. She was being a mother the best way she knew how to a kid like me. She was relentless on trying to find ways to connect with me, but nothing really ever worked. For the most part, that was my fault. I didn't want to let her in. I liked my little bubble I put around myself. I was safe in it.

The truth was that I wanted to connect with my parents. I wanted to be close to them. They were basically the only people in my life that I could really talk to, yet we rarely ever talked about anything.

As time went on, I got more comfortable with the words from my daydreams, so I thought I'd try to use them around my parents once again to see how they would react. To my shock and surprise, my mother played right along. She seemed excited about this game, eager to learn these words. When I would use them, she would try and decipher them first. And if she couldn't, she would ask what the words meant.

Soon enough, we were speaking my new language to each other as though there was nothing odd about it. Like when I asked my mom if I could have ice cream for my **LEMBOT***.

"Ice cream?" she replied. "I guess. But you have to do your **PALLYGO*** and **MACAMOO*** your room first. It's a pigsty in there."

My father, on the other hand, wasn't quite as willing to partake in this madness. It took him some time listening to my mother and I first before he decided to join in. I think he was starting to feel left out and that bothered him. He was seeing how my mother and I interacted with this and he wanted to be a part of it. I needed to give him something that would get him to talk to me and I was hoping he would use this to bridge the gap between us.

Finally, one night during dinner he chimed in with a laugh and said to my mother and I, while we were talking in the new language, "You two are just pawgull!" My mother and I looked at him and just laughed. We sat at the table that night for a long time just talking in this new language. My father became interested and wanted to know more, so I taught him more words. That was the most we all talked together at one time, and for the first time in a long time, I felt like we were a family.

The word pawgull became my father's favorite new word and the only word he would use from my new language. It didn't matter to me if he used one word or all of them. What mattered was that he made the effort to show me he cared.

As I continued to make up this language, I had created countless pages of new words. It was towards the end of summer when I decided to put these words in a small white journal where I would not only write down the words, but their meanings too. Anytime I would remember a new word from my daydreams, I would add that word in the journal. I called this journal **THE DILBONARY***, which I wrote in big red marker on the cover. Of course it had to be red! I mean, what other color would I have used?

The Dilbonary consisted of 100 pages, but I only used 52 pages for the words. I gave each letter of the alphabet two pages to fill up with words. I marked the first page of each letter on the first line on the left side with its letter, sort of like a dictionary.

At that time, I had written down at least one or more words for almost every letter except for A, O, and U, giving me a total of exactly 66 words in the Dilbonary, including the definition of each word. I was proud of the journal and excited about each and every word that was in it. But what was even more exciting to me was all the new words that were still to come.

The first thing that I ever wrote inside the Dilbonary was the word **GIDLADER*** which would eventually be the nickname bestowed upon me by Riley Rogers, the school **JINBONE***.

It was the night before the first day of 6th grade and I had thought long and hard about the Dilbonary and whether or not I should bring it to school. I knew that if any of the other kids found out what it was, I would be ridiculed and teased more than I already had been.

So I made up three rules to help me ensure it didn't fall across the eyes and into the hands of nosy kids, particularly Riley Rogers.

RULE #1: Do not leave the Dilbonary unattended. That meant I couldn't leave the classroom during class, not even to go to the bathroom, no matter how bad I had to go.

RULE #2: Avoid Riley and his band of no-gooders, Johnny and Billy, at all cost.

Capture is death.

RULE #3: Never ever look through the Dilbonary in school. Keep it hidden and out of sight.

It was simple, really. Abide by the rules and no one would know.

But nothing is as simple as we think it is.

CHAPTER 6

KIDS OF THE SQUARE TABLE

It was the first day of 6th grade and I woke up nervous and uneasy. Not because it was the first day of school, which is always intolerable, but I made the decision to bring the Dilbonary to school.

I got dressed, ate breakfast, packed my secret journal in my new red backpack, and headed off to school. I only lived a few streets away from school so my parents let me walk there, which I liked because it gave me time to think about stuff.

When I arrived at the school, I saw Mr. Foster, my 4th grade teacher, standing on the front steps doing door duty as he always does in the mornings. I liked Mr. Foster. He was one of the few teachers who always talked to me, not to mention he had saved me a few times from Riley before he did something cruel to me.

Mr. Foster always wore a tight v-neck t-shirt with black jeans and boots and a black fanny pack where he kept his glasses.

"Hey Mr. Foster," I said to him, waving.

"Hey, welcome back, Dilby," Mr. Foster replied. "What's in your backpack?"

"What?" I said as I tripped going up the stairs, falling on my hands as my backpack went flying off my shoulders, landing next to his feet.

Panic set in as I scrambled to get to my backpack, but it was already in the hands of Mr. Foster.

"You alright, Dilby?" Mr. Foster asked as he helped me up.

"Yeah, I'm fine," I said. "What did you just ask me?" I said nervously.

"I said, nice new backpack," Mr. Foster said as he handed me my backpack. "What did you think I said?"

"Um, nothing, but thanks," I replied as I grabbed it from him.

I was so worried about the Dilbonary that I had misinterpreted what Mr. Foster had actually said. I was freaking myself out and it was making me more nervous about having the Dilbonary with me.

"Better hustle, bell is about to ring," Mr. Foster said as he began to motion the rest of the kids to get inside.

I quickly gathered myself and entered through the school doors just as the bell started ringing. I dodged and weaved my way down the crowded hall to my classroom as I held my backpack tight against my chest with both arms wrapped around it, like I was carrying a bag full of money, guarding it with my life.

I rushed into my classroom, hung up my backpack on the rack, and planted myself in a desk marked with my name on it just as the bell stopped ringing.

The desks in the classroom were set up into three big square tables consisting of eight desks per square that faced each other. My desk was in square 1, the closest to Mrs. Weaver, and one of the middle desks next to Harold who already occupied his desk on the end.

Almost everyone in 6th grade knew Harold. Not because he was popular, but because his mom worked in the school cafeteria, which he used to get teased about. He was kind of nerdy and mostly wore clothes that didn't match very well and always had his shirt tucked in. He was rather shy and really didn't talk much either, like me, however, we would say a few words to each other in class and on occasion at lunch or recess.

There was one thing about my seating position that I liked, and that was that I was second closest to Mrs. Weaver. Being close to her provided me some comfort and safety from kids if I daydreamed.

Mrs. Weaver was an older teacher who liked structure and discipline in her class. She didn't put up with any shenanigans or misbehavior from kids. Her teaching attire consisted of long skirts, blouses, and button up sweaters. She always pulled her hair back and had on her reading glasses that were connected to a thin string around her neck so she always knew where they were when she took them off.

Next to me on my left was Donnie. Next to him on the end was a new student. His name on the desk said Lamont and that's all I knew of him. The desk next to Lamont was empty. Next to the empty desk was Bella. Next to her was Riley Rogers who was directly across from me. And next to Riley was Delia. Riley was without a doubt the worst thing about the square. Of all the desks in the room, Mrs. Weaver had to go and put him facing me. Riley looked over to me and smiled as he cracked his knuckles.

"Well, well, well, this is going to be fun," Riley said with a disturbing little laugh.

Riley was who I feared the most in the whole school, who a lot of kids feared the most. He wore dark colored clothes and leather bracelets on each wrist. He had short, blonde, spiked hair and a small mole next to his nose.

Riley and his no-good friends, Johnny and Billy, were always doing stupid things and making fun of anyone who was scared of them or less popular, which needless to say, I was one of the many that fell into that category.

Today was no exception to that rule as I found out when I reached in to my desk to pull out my work folder. I noticed it had been stuffed with trash and all the books and folders and pencils were moved around and completely disorganized. I looked up at Riley as he looked back at me smirking and giggling at his joke. This was typical stuff that Riley would do, but what could I have done? He was bigger and meaner and I wasn't the type of person to challenge or fight him.

There was no doubt in my mind that he was my biggest concern about the Dilbonary being discovered.

For the first half of the day, I was rather relieved that no one had messed with me. The other kids had stayed clear of me, leaving me alone with the Dilbonary that was stashed safely inside my backpack on the rack. However, every now and then I would check my backpack to make sure it was still there, as if someone somehow went in there when I wasn't looking and took it, even though they didn't know it was in there or even what it was. Yes, I was a little paranoid and protective of it. I had to be; the risk of discovery was too high.

The lunchtime bell finally rang and it couldn't have come at a better time. Of course, I had to use the bathroom like an hour earlier, but I couldn't break one of my rules on the first day. I waited for everyone to leave the room before I grabbed my sack lunch and the Dilbonary out of my backpack. Since I couldn't take my backpack during lunch, I had no choice other than to bring the Dilbonary with me. It was risky but I couldn't leave it unattended in the room.

I shoved the Dilbonary inside my jeans behind my back and pulled my shirt down over it to hide it. I then followed Mrs. Weaver out the room and made a beeline to the bathroom.

When I finally got to the cafeteria, I found an open seat at a table near the back. I really wasn't paying that much attention to who was at the table when I sat down. The table suddenly went quiet as I quickly came to realize that I had sat down at the pop girls table and they made it known real fast that I wasn't welcome there. The first girl to say something was Delia, who was sitting across from me.

Delia was a pop girl as well as a glamourpuss, which is to say she was popular and dressed for attention and cared way more about what people thought about her appearance than she did. She had dark brown curly hair that was always pulled back in a tight ponytail, except for last year on picture day when she let it down and straightened it to try to make herself look more mature. It looked ridiculous if you asked me. She was rather snobbish and dressed in trendy stylish clothes and always had her nails painted in bright colors and even wore make-up. Delia never talked to me unless she absolutely had to.

This was one of those times.

"Umm, what are you doing?" Delia said with some attitude.

"Just eating lunch," I responded, as all the girls snickered at my response.

"Not here, you're not!" Delia enforced upon me. "This is the pop girls table and you're not a girl and you sure aren't popular, so find somewhere else to eat."

"Yeah, you're totally bothering us," Hailey said.

Hailey is a wannabe Delia. She tries to dress, act, talk, and look like Delia, but falls short. It annoys Delia, but she kind of likes it as well.

I looked around the table as all the girls were giving me disgusted looks, like I just picked my nose or something.

"But I'm not doing anything," I said. "I'm just quietly sitting here."

"Yeah, well, that's annoying us, okay," Delia said.

"Seriously?" I said.

"Yeah, seriously," Delia said.

"Would you mind just maybe finding another table to sit at please, you know, girl privacy and all," Bella said in a nice sweet tone. "We would really appreciate that."

Sitting next to Delia was Bella, who also was a pop girl, perhaps the most liked girl in my grade. She always knew how to make something she said sound nice and sweet, even though it was meant to be mean and hurtful. She was smart, pretty, and nice and she was always well dressed in fashionable clothes which consisted mainly of dresses and matching shoes with heels. She had long light brown hair that went down the middle of her back and shined like gold when the light hit it just right. The teachers and kids all liked her because she was always polite and respectful in and outside of class. However, she too never spoke to me unless she had to.

Though Bella and Delia's personalities and fashion choices might have been different, they'd been best friends since the 2nd grade. They were inseparable, always gossiping and passing notes in class. They were known around the school as the Glam Duo.

"Sure," I said, unenthusiastically.

"Thanks," Bella said.

I gathered my lunch and walked off trying to ignore the whispering remarks the girls were saying about me. I was over the notion of having lunch in the cafeteria, so I trashed my lunch and made my way back to the classroom.

As I was walking down the hall back to the classroom, I noticed I couldn't feel the Dilbonary poking me in my back anymore. I reached around to feel for it but it wasn't there. Instant panic set in. I lost the Dilbonary!

Nooo!

It fell out somewhere and I didn't even notice. I immediately looked around me but it wasn't anywhere in sight. I quickly retraced my steps back down the hall and into the cafeteria, but I found nothing.

I scanned over the lunch tables to see if someone had it, but no one did that I could see. I had to find it before someone else did. I was like a crazed lunatic scurrying between the tables looking everywhere as I headed toward the back where I was sitting at the pop girls table. I stopped and walked slowly trying to be inconspicuous and not draw attention to myself as I made my way around the table to the spot I was sitting at.

Oh my crap! There it was, lying on the ground under the bench seat facing up, exposing the words, The Dilbonary.

It was apparent that no one had noticed it on the ground. The pop girls must have been too caught up in their mindless discussion of girl talk that they failed to see the Dilbonary laying on the floor.

I was steadfast and stealthy in my movements, like a ninja, as I bent down and took hold of the Dilbonary without anyone seeing.

"Uh, what are you doing back here?" Delia said. "I thought we told you to leave?"

"You did... I am," I said as I slid the Dilbonary under my shirt behind my back, hiding it as I stood there breathing heavy.

"Well...then go," Hailey said.

"What a weirdo," I heard Delia say as I made like lighting and bolted away from them and headed out of the cafeteria with the Dilbonary stashed behind my back.

As I entered the hall, I ran into Grace Billings walking by. She looked different than last year. Her brown hair was much longer and stringy now and parted down the middle. She wore a pair of black-rimmed glasses that rested just below her eyes on the middle of her nose. She had on blue jeans with bellbottoms, an orange loose t-shirt, an over-sized green hoodie that was unzipped, and fuzzy brown boots that looked like slippers. She also had a gold watch with a worn brown leather band on her left wrist.

"Hey, watch where you're...oh, hey Dilby," Grace said with a welcoming smile.

"Hh, hhi Grace," I said, stammering my words.

I was nervously fidgeting as I stood with my hands behind my back holding the Dilbonary.

"You okay?" Grace asked, taking notice of my demeanor. "You need help with something?"

"No, I'm, I'm good." I said.

An awkward silence came between us. I was uncomfortable and I wanted to go.

"I gotta get to class," I said as I left her standing there alone.

"Bye!" Grace shouted out.

I got to the classroom as fast as I could and stood against the wall with my back to it. I took a deep breath and let out a sigh of relief knowing the Dilbonary was safe. I was lucky this time as my carelessness almost led to the discovery of my secret journal. I must have been distracted by the pop girls insensitivity to me that I didn't realize the Dilbonary had fallen out from behind my back. I lost focus, something I couldn't afford to lose again.

Time seemed to go by so slowly as I waited for Mrs. Weaver to return so I could go inside and put the Dilbonary safely back inside my backpack. As I leaned against the wall, I watched as teachers and kids walked past me never looking at me or saying a word to me as though I wasn't even there. There wasn't a "are you waiting for someone" or "do you need something" from any teachers. Not even a "hey loser" or "freak" from any kids. I got nothing. I was like a ghost.

Since I started school, I didn't try and stand out, but I didn't want to be invisible either. That's how I felt most of the time, as though I didn't exist at school. For the most part, I accepted my social status as a loner or the pawgull kid. But every now and then I felt the urge and wished that I could just fit in. I wanted to be like the cool kids, but for me, reaching that status seemed impossible.

For the next few months, nothing changed.

As the end of the first half of the school year was approaching, I managed to stay under the radar of Riley and the no-gooders while up holding my rules of the Dilbonary, keeping it exclusive to my eyes only. It was hard, but I did it and no one suspected a thing.

Then, a few days before my 11th birthday, I faltered and the rules began to crumble.

CHAPTER 7

BREAKING ALL THE RULES

It was a cold morning as I walked up to the school playground. Having gotten there 20 minutes before school started, there were only a few kids meandering about in the yard playing sports and just goofing off. I looked around and spotted a lonely tree off in the distance and decided to go give it some company. I sat down behind the tree facing the other way trying to hide myself from anyone.

I had a dream the night before where I had new words that I had forgotten to write in the Dilbonary. I wanted to write them in there before I forgot again but I didn't want to expose the Dilbonary as rule #3 states. But the excitement of the words and the Dilbonary was getting to me and I badly wanted to take it out. I told myself I would be really fast, in and out, and no one would see. I had a lack of willpower and so against my better judgement, I took the Dilbonary out.

I peeked around the tree and scanned the playground for any nearby curious kids, more importantly, Riley and the no-gooders. The coast looked clear and no one was around or even close to me. I quickly unzipped my backpack and took out the Dilbonary, placing it on top of my lap. I grabbed a pencil, opened it up, and began to add each new word onto the appropriate letter page. I wrote **BITPOG*** under the "B" section, then flipped to the "Y" section where I wrote **YOUPP***.

I was trying to move as fast as I could but it was hard to rush what made me happy. I enjoyed this so much to the point it consumed me and I would block out all that was around me. That's why I failed to notice or hear George walk up from behind and stand over me.

"What's that?" George said.

My heart jumped and I quickly closed the Dilbonary. I then looked up to see George hovering over me focused on the journal.

Kaboom! Rule #3 just got blown up.

George and I barely knew or spoke to each other and we weren't exactly friends but rather just friendly to each other. He was a science geek and smart as a whip.

"What's the dil-bon-air-ee?" George said as he was sounding it out.

I looked back down, realizing he had seen the title on the cover.

"It's nothing," I said as I shoved the book back in my backpack and got up from the ground.

"It doesn't look like nothing," George said. "Come on, tell me, what is it?"

"Really, it's nothing. Just some stupid thing I did, that's all," I said.

"Well, what's in it?" George said.

"Nothing," I replied as I started to walk off.

But George wasn't giving up that easy and he walked step by step with me.

"Then what's it mean?" George asked. "Your name is Dilby and it said Dilbonary on it. So what is it?"

I kept my mouth closed and just kept walking, hoping he'd stop.

"Oh, I know, it's some secret code book or something, right?" George said with excitement. "Wait, are you a spy?"

I quickly stopped. I turned and leaned into him.

"No, George, I'm not a spy and it's not a code book," I said quietly. "Like I told you, it's nothing, really."

I then walked away.

"You are a spy, I knew it!" George said aloud.

I tucked my head down and quickly picked up the pace as I made my getaway to the school door before anyone could say anything.

Once I got inside the school, I headed straight to the bathroom and locked myself inside a stall. I was terrified. I had exposed the Dilbonary and now everyone was going to know. If only I had left my secret journal at home or perhaps not written "The Dilbonary" in big red marker on the front, George would not have known what it was or even cared. How could I have been so careless? Why did I do something so stupid like that? I knew better than to risk it, and now I was going to pay the price.

I stayed hidden in the stall for the next few minutes as kids came and went. I kept thinking Riley would come in and find me and then it would be over for sure, but he never came. The stench in the stall was becoming overwhelming so I cracked open the stall door just to make sure no one was there. The coast was clear so I left the stall and rushed out.

When I swung open the bathroom door and stepped into the hallway, I bumped right into Riley and his band of no-good-ers passing by. I instinctively grabbed my backpack.

And down went Rule #2!

"Well, well, well, look who it is," Riley said as he and the no-gooders surrounded me.

I looked around as I tried to escape, but there was nowhere to run. They had blocked me in.

"Where you going in such a hurry?" Riley asked.

"Nowhere," I said.

"You wouldn't be trying to hide from me now, would ya?" Riley said as he stepped closer to me.

"Hide?" I said nervously, stammering my words. "Why, why would I be trying to hide? I'm just going to class."

"Because you have something that I want," Riley said.

"Yeah, you have something," Johnny said.

Johnny was smaller than Riley but he was heavier. He wore long jean shorts and shirts that were a bit too small for him with black sneakers and socks that almost went to his knees. He had short dark curly hair that always looked messy.

"Yeah, and Riley wants it," Billy said.

Billy was the runt of the group. He was short and skinny and had no distinct clothing style as he wore just about anything and everything. His hair was blonde and short, almost like a buzz cut, except for the front, which was longer and flipped up.

"But I don't have anything, I swear," I pleaded.

"So you don't have a book called the dilben...the drilbon... what it's called?" Riley said as he slapped Billy on the arm.

"Dilbonry, I think," Billy said.

"Is it dilbony?" Johnny said.

Riley was getting frustrated that they couldn't remember the name.

"Well, whatever it's called, hand it over," Riley said.

"But I don't have anything," I said.

Riley grabbed hold of my backpack and pushed me up against the wall.

"Give it up or I'm gonna mess you up," Riley said with his tough guy tone.

I gripped my backpack as hard as I could and closed my eyes, waiting for the beat down from Riley.

"Hey, let him go, Riley," I heard a voice say.

I opened my eyes as Donnie Palmer approached us. Riley released his grip and backed away from me as he squared up to Donnie.

Donnie was a **SPINHOOT*** and a little bigger than Riley was. He was always playing sports and wearing some kind of sports team shirt with bright colors. He was always nice and cool with almost everyone, except for Riley and the no-gooders. He didn't like jinbones and Riley and the no-gooders didn't like spinhoots, which was why they always butted heads. Donnie always stuck up for the kids who couldn't defend themselves, which was why he was so well liked by the girls, especially Delia, who everyone knew had a crush on him.

"Well, look who came to save the loser?" Riley said.

"Don't you ever have anything better to do than pick on people?" Donnie said.

"Like what, play football?" Riley said as he made a goofy football gesture of throwing a pass.

"Yeah, go long Donnie," Johnny said.

"Yeah, get that touchdown," Billy said.

Riley looked to Billy and pushed him.

"Shut up, stupid," Riley said to Billy as he put his head down and looked away like a dog that just got yelled at.

"Come on Dilby, let's go," Donnie said.

"No way, jock boy," Riley said as he put his hand on my chest to stop me from leaving. "He's got something that he was just about to give me."

"I told you, I don't have anything," I said.

"He says he doesn't have anything, so back off Riley," Donnie said as he stepped up to Riley.

"Always coming to the rescue, aren't you jocky," Riley said.

"Always trying to be a tough guy, aren't you spiky," Donnie replied.

I couldn't help but let out a little laugh of Donnie's crack at Riley's hair.

"Oh, that's funny?" Riley said looking at me. "I'll come find you later, loser boy."

Riley stared down Donnie as he and the no-gooders walked off down the hallway.

"You alright?" Donnie asked.

Yeah, I'm fine." I said. "Thanks Donnie."

"Why do you let him push you around like that?" Donnie said. "You gotta stand up to him sometime."

"Yeah, okay," I said.

It might be easy for Donnie to stand up to jinbones, but I'm not like that. I'd sooner run away before I fought Riley.

"See ya," I said as I nodded at Donnie and then took my speedy leave from the scene of the accident and headed to class.

I may have broken a rule but I still had the Dilbonary. All was not lost thanks to Donnie, but the battle with Riley had just begun.

Things were about to change and that day would turn into one of the worst and best days I ever had at school so far.

CHAPTER 8

THE CAT'S OUT OF THE BAG

The school bell was ringing when I rushed into my classroom and planted myself at my desk, barely making it on time. Normally, backpacks get hung up on the wall after you've taken out your folder and books before the bell rings, but since I was late and had no time to take out my stuff, I had to keep it under my desk.

This was actually a good thing, I thought at the moment, because I was able to keep it close to me, especially with Riley staring at me from across the desk.

The day continued on and all was as normal as it could be at the square table. We had just finished our math worksheets and Mrs. Weaver was just about to give the class a writing assignment when her school phone rang.

"Hello...okay, great. Thank you," Mrs. Weaver said.

She hung up the phone as everyone quickly looked away.

"Who would like to go the front office and pick something up for me?" Mrs. Weaver asked.

The class was silent and no one said anything or even raised a hand. Normally, I liked to help Mrs. Weaver because

I liked her, but not today. I couldn't risk leaving the Dilbonary alone in the backpack under my desk near the grabby hands of a suspicious jinbone. So I stayed quiet and kept my head down.

"Nobody wants to go?" Mrs. Weaver said. "Okay, I guess I'll just have to pick someone to be my little helper."

NO, not her little helper! I sooo did not want to be Mrs. Weaver's little helper. Nobody wanted to be Mrs. Weaver's little helper. The name alone is just embarrassing and humiliating, something that will surely haunt your existence in school and never be forgotten.

"PLEASE don't pick me, please!" I remembered praying.

But what happened if she did? I couldn't take my backpack with me and I couldn't hang it up at the backpack rack. And I certainly couldn't take the Dilbonary out to bring with me because everyone would see it. I was freaking out!

Mrs. Weaver looked around the room, searching for her perfect little helper.

"Let's see...," she said.

"Please don't be me...please don't be me...please don't be me," I repeated in my head like a mantra as I squeezed my eyes closed so hard I thought they were going to burst.

"Dilby," she said aloud.

"NOOOOOOOOOOOOOOO!" I silently screamed in my head.

I let out a deep sigh as I opened my eyes, knowing what was to come.

"Would you go to the front office and pick up an envelope for me, please. Thank you," Mrs. Weaver said, as a few of the kids chuckled.

"But Mrs. Weaver, do I have to go?" I pleaded.

"Well, you can ask if anyone else wants to go instead of you," Mrs. Weaver said.

I looked around the class, as everyone was head down and quiet. I knew no one would take my place, but I had to ask. I had to get out of not going.

"Would anybody want to go to the office for me?" I asked in a pathetic, whimpy kind of way.

The room remained quiet and no one even looked up or answered.

"Well, I think you have your answer, Dilby," Mrs. Weaver said. "The office is waiting for you, thank you."

I was doomed. I had no choice but to break Rule #1.

I couldn't believe that in just one day I broke all three rules. What I thought would be simple was far from it. It was a nightmare.

"Hurry back, little helper," Riley whispered as he leaned over his desk to me and laughed with a silly smirk on his face.

I pushed the chair back away from my desk, looked at my backpack like I was leaving it forever, got up, and headed out of the classroom. I could hear everyone giggling at me as I passed by them. Why Mrs. Weaver made me her "little helper" today of all days is beyond me. If only she knew what that would do to me.

I thought I was one of her good students. I thought she liked me. I was always well behaved in class, never got in trouble, and always got my work done. Apparently, I thought wrong.

Time was critical so I hustled through the halls to the front office where I picked up the envelope from Ms. Beasley, the secretary. But before I left, I saw George sitting in a chair. I knew I had to hurry back but I had a bone to pick with him so

I walked over and stood in front of him. He didn't look so good sitting there as his eyes were closed and he was sort of swaying side to side holding onto a paper bag.

"You alright there, George?" I asked.

George opened his eyes and looked up at me with a little squint.

"I don't feel so good," George said.

"Well, that makes two of us," I said. "Why did you tell Riley about my journal?"

"You mean the Dilbonary?" George said as he struggled to get the words out.

"You don't even know what it is," I said. "You shouldn't have told him."

"I didn't," George said.

Just then, Nurse Lynn came over. "Hey George, come with me and we'll see what's wrong, okay?" Nurse Lynn put her arm around George and began to lead him away.

"Then who did you tell?" I asked.

"I think I'm going to be sick," George said to Nurse Lynn as they disappeared into her office.

It was clear that George, Riley, and the no-gooders weren't the only ones that knew about the Dilbonary and it seemed that word of it was quickly spreading. But who did George tell if it wasn't Riley?

With the envelope still in hand, I booked it out of the front office and hightailed it back to the classroom. I stopped in front of the door as I looked in through the glass panels. All seemed normal, as everyone was head down into their work.

I took a deep breath, opened the door, and headed inside. When I entered, everyone looked up at me and watched me like hawks as I quickly made my way to Mrs. Weaver and handed her the envelope. When I turned to go back to my seat, I saw everyone was head down again into their work.

When I pulled out my chair to sit, I noticed that my backpack was flat on the floor. Before I left the classroom, it was leaning up. It was at that moment my life flashed before my eyes.

I quickly sat down, grabbed it, and looked inside. Luckily, the Dilbonary was still there but I could tell that it had been moved around. It was upside down and placed on top rather than hidden at the bottom. My heart raced and I became short of breath. The unimaginable had happened. The Dilbonary had been discovered, and most likely by the worst person to do so, Riley Rogers. The rest of my life was over. I would be ridiculed for eternity.

I hid the Dilbonary back behind the stuff in my backpack and zipped it up. Everyone was still head down except Riley, who just stared over at me like I was his prey. Time seemed to stand still as he leaned over, paused just before reaching my desk, and whispered, "gidlader."

My heart stopped and I felt sick to my stomach. I wanted to run away and never come back. My mind became occupied with scenarios of what Riley would do.

I pictured Riley and his band of no-good friends waiting for me after school where they would take the Dilbonary from me and read it out loud, while everyone laughed at me. I even went as far as imagining Riley ripping up the journal into pieces and then, since it's Riley, he would then eat the paper just so I could never have it again.

My blood started to boil and I got mad. I looked at Riley who was laughing back at me. I wanted to be the jinbone and teach him a lesson. Then, with one brave move I jumped across the desk and threw him down to the ground. I pinned his arms down with my legs, restraining him. I picked up a pair of scissors from the ground nearby and began to cut his spiked hair off one spike at a time as I laughed aloud like a crazy person as Riley began to cry. All the kids were laughing and pointing at him. I sat atop him reveling in my victory as I threw his hair up in the air.

"Dilby," I heard Harold say quietly as I could feel a nudge on my arm. "Dilby, snap out of it."

I blinked my eyes and came to. I looked across at Riley who was staring back, realizing I had fantasized about cutting Riley's hair off.

"Where'd ya go, gidlader?" Riley whispered. "Another stupid dream?"

Riley laughed softly and then went back to his assignment.

I turned to Harold. "Thanks," I said.

Harold nodded and went back to his work.

For the rest of the morning, I couldn't concentrate on anything else. Schoolwork became unimportant to me and paying attention to Mrs. Weaver became a thing of the past. I knew that the discovery of the Dilbonary was going to be another chapter of torture carried out by Riley and his band of no-gooders.

I was losing my mind over this and it was consuming me more and more as time went on. Riley could see what this was doing to me and he was enjoying every moment of it. He just sat there waiting for that bell to ring so he could do to me what he had always wanted to do.

I tried to figure out a way to escape, but I had nothing. Riley was going to get to me one way or another and there was no way to avoid it. All I could do was try to delay the inevitable and prepare myself for the worst.

The lunch bell sounded but I had no appetite whatsoever and my stomach was in knots. I felt like George did and wanted to just throw up. All I could think about was Riley and the Dilbonary and what was going to happen.

Avoiding the cafeteria was a no-brainer so I realized that finding a safe hiding place during lunch was the key to avoiding Riley and his band of no-gooders. So I decided to go to the one place he would never go, the library.

I waited until everyone left the classroom to go to lunch before I retreated there.

CHAPTER 9

MY SAVING GRACE

When I entered the library it was empty of kids. Even the librarian wasn't there as she usually was. I didn't think too much about it and took to a secluded corner of the room and nestled into a beanbag chair. I clutched my backpack and rested it on my lap as I sat all alone listening to the buzzing sound of the florescent lights that provided the only sound in the room.

My safe little spot in the library felt like the only place I could breath and let my guard down. I could relax in peace without having to constantly look over my shoulder for the onslaught of the Riley brigade.

It was no more than a few minutes after I had sat down in the beanbag that I heard the library door open and then close. I froze and just sat silently. My first thought was that Riley had found me. This was it. I was done for! There was nowhere for me to run and hide. The time had come for me to face him and take what was coming.

I held my breath and listened closely, but there were no voices, only the soft footsteps of someone making their way through the room, heading toward my direction. I wanted to hide the Dilbonary but I couldn't, on account of making too much noise, which would give away my position. I covered it the best I could with my hands and just waited for what was to come.

The footsteps got closer and closer to me. Suddenly, the footsteps stopped.

"Dilby, you in here?" I heard a girl's voice say.

Then, from behind the bookshelf of the aisle, a girl peeked her head around the corner and locked eyes with me. It was Grace.

"There you are," Grace said as she stepped out into full view and stood in front of me.

We looked at each other for a moment before she made her way over to my corner and stood looking down at me. I quickly slid the Dilbonary inside my backpack, hoping she wouldn't notice, but it was obvious she could see I was trying to hide something.

Aside from the watermelon incident a year before, every now and then our paths would cross in the halls or playground and we would say "hi" but that was the extent of our friendship, if you could even call it that. And never had she sought me out. This indeed was a first and it had me curious.

"Hey Dilby," Grace said. She nervously played with her glasses.

"Hey Grace," I replied while shifting around in the bean-bag. I was a little nervous, too.

A moment of uncomfortable silence passed before she sat down next to me, leaning back against the bookshelf.

"Sooo whatcha doin'?" Grace asked.

"Nothing, really," I responded.

I wasn't sure why she was there or what she even wanted, and her presence had made me a bit uneasy.

"How did you know I was here?" I asked.

"I saw you walk in here so I followed you," Grace said. "And when you didn't come back out, I thought I'd come in here to find you."

"Find me for what?" I asked.

"Well...I was hoping I could see it?" Grace asked quietly.

I pushed myself up in the beanbag and pulled my backpack closer to me.

"See...see what?" I said as if I didn't know what she was talking about.

"You know...that book you have," Grace said, with excitement in her voice.

"It's not a book, it's a journal," I said without thinking, realizing I just told her I had something. "And how do you know about...oh, yeah, of course... Riley," I said unenthusiastically.

"Riley didn't tell me," Grace said.

"Then how did you know about it?" I asked.

"George told me," Grace said.

"And then you told Riley, right?" I said.

"No way, I would never tell Riley anything," Grace said.

"So then who did you talk about it to?" I asked.

"No one," Grace said. "I swear."

"Then who told Riley?" I asked.

"Beats me," Grace said.

I sat there confused. I didn't know what to think. Was Grace lying about this or was George?

"Well, I'd still love to see the journal. It sounds super cool," Grace said.

"Why? So you can make fun of me too?" I said rudely.

"Why would I do that? Like I said, it sounds super cool," Grace said.

"And why should I believe you?" I said.

Grace turned and leaned into me.

"I won't, I promise," Grace pleaded. "And I won't tell anyone you showed me either or about this cool hiding spot you have."

I wasn't sure I could trust her. We weren't friends, but then again, she had never done or said anything mean to me. She herself had been made fun of over and over and even had a horrible nickname. After promising myself that I would keep the Dilbonary a secret, deep down I truly did want to tell somebody. I just didn't know who I could trust.

"Pleeeease Dilby, I really want to see it," Grace said, almost begging me to show her. "And I swear, cross my heart I won't tell anybody." She crossed her heart with her fingers.

I looked down at my backpack where the Dilbonary was and then back up at Grace who was waiting in anticipation for my answer.

"I don't know, Grace," I said, unsure of what to do.

"If I ever tell anyone, you can yell out 'Brace Face Grace' in front of everybody every time you see me," Grace said.

I just looked at her knowing I would never do that regardless of what happened. I stood up and looked around the library to see if anyone else was there. It was empty except for Grace and me. I looked at the clock on the wall and saw there was about 15 minutes left until lunch ended. After a few moments of serious thought, I decided to let Grace see my most prized possession. I sat back down on the beanbag, reached in my backpack, and pulled out my secret journal, holding it in my hands. Grace's eyes widened when she saw it.

"So that's the book everyone's talking about?" Grace asked anxiously.

"It's a journal. And everyone's talking about it?" I said rather shocked, even though I knew word had gotten around. I just didn't expect it to be that fast.

Grace just grinned and nodded her head up and down.

"Sooo...can I see it?" Grace asked, ever so nicely.

At this point, I really didn't have anything to lose by not showing her, and after all, I really did want to show somebody. And who better to give it to than someone who didn't make fun of me and who was an outcast like me?

I wasn't very confident or secure about sharing the Dilbonary with anyone, but Grace somehow made me feel otherwise about her. I exhaled deeply and handed it to her like I was presenting her with some rare diamond.

Grace took the Dilbonary and placed it onto her lap. I sank back into the beanbag and sat there watching her look at it. Her eyes got big and a smile formed on her face with each turn of the pages.

"This is sooo cool, Dilby," Grace said. "I mean **SMOONEYS***, that is so cute!"

Cute wasn't exactly the word I was hoping for, but I'd take it as a compliment. For the next ten minutes or so, we sat together talking about it as she scanned through the Dilbonary. Discussing my journal with her made me think maybe I was overreacting about kids seeing it. Maybe kids wouldn't make fun of it or me and they'd find it just as exciting as I did. But still, I wasn't ready to share this with anyone else.

She finished looking through the journal, closed it, and handed it back to me just as I had presented it to her. I took it and placed it safely back inside my backpack.

"The Dilbonary...is awesome," Grace said with a smile. "How did you ever come up with those words?"

"You won't believe me if I told you," I said.

"Sure I would," Grace said. "Come on tell me, I'm dying to know now."

"Are you just saying that or do you really want to know?"

"Yes, I really want to know," Grace said.

I looked away from her, feeling a little embarrassed.

"I get them from my dreams," I said softly.

"You mean the dreams you're always having?" Grace said.

"Yeah, I come up with them in my dreams and I remember them," I said.

"You must have some crazy dreams," Grace said with a giggle.

"You have no idea," I said.

"What do you mean?" Grace said, as she seemed even more intrigued.

I sat up and leaned in to her.

"Well, my dreams...they're real!" I said quietly. "I call them time dreams."

Just then, the school bell rang out signifying lunch was over. I jumped up and looked at the clock.

"Wait, what do you mean they're real?" Grace said. "And what's a time dream?"

"I gotta go, I don't want to run into Riley in the hall," I said as I grabbed my backpack and started to walk away. Grace got up behind me and quickly followed me, wanting to hear more.

"Real, like as in...real real?" Grace whispered.

I reached the door, stopped, and turned around to her.

"Yeah, like real real!" I whispered back as I opened the door and walked out.

I expected Grace to be right on my heels firing more questions at me, but she wasn't. I wondered if she had thought I was messing with her because the expression on her face when I left her looked as though she had just been tricked. I didn't have time to wait and explain more so I booked it down the hall toward my classroom.

As I was scurrying down the hallway, a voice echoed out from behind me. "Dilby!"

I turned around and saw Grace standing in the distance.

"I believe you," Grace yelled out, followed by a smile.

CHAPTER 10

RUN, DILBY, RUN

The school bell rang ending the day and all I thought about since lunchtime in the library was Grace. She was different than the other kids in school, which is probably why I showed her the Dilbonary. There was something about her that made me feel like I could trust her and call her my friend.

As I made my way out the double doors to the front of the school, I saw Grace sitting on the wall of the front steps.

"Hey, Grace," I said.

"Hi, Dilby," Grace replied.

"You waiting for someone?" I asked.

"Yeah, my mom, she picks me up," Grace said. "I was also hoping I'd see you before I left. I wanted to say thanks for letting me see (she mouthed the words) the Dilbonary. It's really cool."

"Well, thanks for not making fun of it," I said.

"So did you ever find out who told Riley?" Grace asked.

"No, not yet," I said.

"I'll ask around for you, see if anyone knows," Grace said.

"Thanks, that'd be really cool," I said.

Just then a horn honked and Grace turned to see her Mom in a car by the curb.

"That's my mom, I gotta go," Grace said. "I'll see ya tomorrow."

"Yeah, see ya," I said.

Before Grace got into the car, she turned and waved to me. I smiled and waved back. I watched Grace drive off then adjusted my backpack on my back and headed off to home.

As I walked down the sidewalk in front of the school, I caught something out of the corner of my eye. I looked over to the school where Riley and the no-gooders were leaning against the wall watching me.

"Awe, did your girlfriend leave you all alone?" Riley said, as I turned away and kept walking. It seemed that Riley and the no-gooders had been watching Grace and I at the wall. I had only hoped he didn't hear anything we talked about.

"Where ya going, gidlader?" Riley said.

"Yeah, where ya going?" Johnny said.

They moved away from the wall and began to come after me. I picked up the pace and walked faster.

"Time's up, loser, I'm coming to get what's mine," Riley said. "No one here to save you now!"

"Yeah, we're coming," Billy said.

"Well, you'll never get it," I said before I burst into an all out run.

"Let's get him," Riley yelled out as they took off after me.

My backpack didn't help matters as it flew from side to side on my back as I sprinted down the sidewalk, throwing me a little off balance.

Riley and the no-gooders were slowly gaining on me.

"You're dead meat, gidlader!" Riley yelled from behind me.

There was no way I could let them catch me. My house wasn't very far away so if I could just get there I'd be safe. My adrenaline kicked in and with my long legs I stretched out my strides, slammed it into overdrive, and flew down the street, widening my distance from Riley and the no-gooders.

I took a glance behind me to see where they were. By the time I turned the corner at the end of the street, they were about two houses away from me.

I can make it, I thought. All I had to do was keep running.

Just as I turned back around, out of nowhere, a little girl on a training bike came flying down her driveway onto the sidewalk in front of me and stopped. I had but a split second to react, leaving me the only option, other than crashing into the girl, of leaping over her. I saw the fear in her face as I planted my right foot in front of her and launched myself in the air.

Instead of jumping with my feet first like you would normally jump, like over hurdle or a jump rope, I did more like a dive over her. My stomach barely brushed against her head as I flew over the tiny girl, superhero style.

I wish I could say I landed cleanly with a sweet tuck and roll, then back on my feet running away like they do in action movies, but I didn't and it wasn't.

It was a disaster from the moment I saw her in front of me.

I was completely off balance when I jumped. As I was flying through the air, I realized it wasn't going to be a pretty landing, and with my arms flailing in front of me, I hoped I would catch my fall and not break both my arms.

The hard ground was approaching fast.

I landed with my right arm taking most of the impact of the fall and rolled onto my right shoulder as the momentum of the landing propelled my body into a sideways roll ending on my back. My backpack still managed to somehow stay on my back, which provided some cushion for me.

Surprisingly, I wasn't really hurt and if I was, my adrenaline was taking care of any pain because I didn't feel anything except for fear and the need to get up and run.

I looked up and saw that Riley and no-gooders had rounded the corner and their sights of catching me were closing in fast.

"There he is, we got him," Riley shouted.

I jumped up to my feet and took off running down the sidewalk as fast I could.

Up ahead I saw a package delivery truck pulling up to a house on the same side of the street I was running on.

At the same time I heard a dog barking from behind me. I turned around and saw a little black dog chasing after me and growling like he wanted to eat me. If Riley wasn't bad enough, now I had a dog chasing me too!

As I approached the truck, the deliveryman stepped out onto the sidewalk from the truck directly in my running path.

Right as I was about to run into him, he looked and saw me barreling down on him. We were headed for a collision.

Then, as though we had rehearsed it, he jumped back out of the way against the truck. His package went flying as I did some crazy spin move that I'd never done before at the exact same time. The timing was impeccable as we narrowly missed crashing into each other. Somehow I maintained my balance and kept on running safely ahead.

I wish I could say the same for the deliveryman. Unfortunately, he was met with the little angry dog that went straight for his pant leg and bit down.

The deliveryman screamed and tried to shake off the dog, taking up the whole sidewalk, flailing around as the little dog held on tight. Riley and the no-gooders pursuit was held up as they slowed down to get around the dog show.

Up on the left was an alleyway that went between two houses that led to the street I lived on. As I headed for it, I looked back and could only see Riley and Johnny chasing after me. Before I could think about what happened to Billy, I saw him running away in the opposite direction of me screaming as the little angry dog was chasing after him.

I entered the alleyway and zigzagged around the steel partitions bars that stood in between the walls of the two houses before I made it through.

All I had to do now was turn the corner onto my street and go six houses and then I'd be home free. But I wasn't out of the woods yet.

As I rounded the corner, I failed to notice the uneven sidewalk as it caught my right foot and sent me tumbling face first into the grass yard of Mr. Bailey.

Mr. Bailey was an older man and kind of a grumpster. He was obsessed about keeping his grass green and well manicured and hated when people walked on it, especially kids.

When I got up, I saw a few books and the Dilbonary lying on the grass in front of me. I didn't realize that my backpack was unzipped, which must've happened when I crash landed over the girl. I quickly gathered up all the books and the Dilbonary and shoved them back into my backpack and zipped it up.

"Johnny, come on man, get up!" I heard Riley's voice coming from around the corner.

"I twisted my ankle on the bar," Johnny yelled back.

I couldn't see Riley but from the sound of his voice, he was close, too close to try and run now. I had to hide, but where?

In the driveway of the house I saw Mr. Bailey's old parked car. It looked high enough off the ground for me to slide under it, but I wasn't sure. At that moment, the car looked like the best choice for cover so I ran over to it. I laid flat on my stomach and wiggled my way underneath. Good thing I was skinny as I fit with a little room to spare.

I tried to control my breathing as I remained quiet and still.

From my vantage point, I could see the corner of the street. Seconds later, Riley came flying around the corner. When he couldn't see me anymore, he stopped. Riley bent over with his hands on his knees trying to catch his breath.

"Where'd ya go, gidlader!" Riley yelled out as he looked around the area.

Johnny came hobbling up behind Riley tiptoeing on his left foot and wincing in pain.

"I think he's gone, Riley," Billy said. " Let's just go."

"No way, he's hiding somewhere and were gonna find him," Riley said. "Come on out, you little freak."

I was like a statue under that car. Any little movement would've given away my position and no way did I want that.

"Look around, he's here somewhere," Riley barked out.

"My ankle hurts really bad so I'm just gonna go home," Johnny said.

"Whatever, be a wuss, Johnny. I'll find him myself," Riley said as he began searching the yard.

Johnny turned and limped off, disappearing into the alleyway.

Riley continued looking behind the bushes by the house on the opposite end of where I was. He was making his way towards the car when the garage door to the house opened up.

I looked toward the garage when I saw Mr. Bailey come out. Riley must've not heard the garage open because I could see the shock on his face as he froze when Mr. Bailey walked out and saw him.

"Hey! What are you doing in my yard?" Mr. Bailey yelled. "And get off my grass!"

"Relax dude, I'm just looking for someone," Riley said.

"Well, look somewhere else before I call the police!" Mr. Bailey said.

"Okay, I'm going," Riley said as he retreated off the grass yard.

Mr. Bailey walked down to the sidewalk, prompting Riley to go.

"Just look at what you did! You ruined my grass!" Mr. Bailey said, distraught over his grass.

"You can't hide forever, gidlader!" Riley yelled out. "I'll find ya' tomorrow."

"Go on, get out of here," Mr. Bailey said.

"And that book is mine!" Riley said as he turned and walked away.

I let out a deep sigh of relief. It seemed I had somehow evaded capture and I lived to see another day. Now all I had to do was wait for Mr. Bailey to go back inside before I could get out from under the car.

But Mr. Bailey didn't go back inside.

Instead, he stood there for a moment looking over at his trampled grass before he walked over, opened up his car door, and got in.

"Dang hooligan, always messing up my grass," I heard Mr. Bailey say just before he shut the door.

Uh oh, this was bad.

I had to get out of there before he started it up and drove away. But I had to do it without getting seen. I quickly scooted my body toward the edge of car where a small wall belonging to the house next door stood a few feet away.

Just as I reached the edge...the car started up.

The loud noise of the motor startled me and I hit my head on the frame of the car above me. Oowww!

I had no time to worry about the pain as I could feel the rumbling of the exhaust pipes as the engine revved up. I took notice that I was right in line with the tires as I heard the car shift into gear and saw it slowly start to move forward.

It was time to move or I would've been squashed. I quickly inched out from under the car, my feet barely missed getting trapped under the back tire, and dove over the wall onto the grass yard next door. I laid there silently until I didn't hear the car anymore as it rumbled down the street.

I peeked over the wall to make sure the coast was clear of Riley just in case he decided to come back. He did not.

I took a moment to collect myself realizing that I had just escaped near death.

I got to my feet, grabbed my backpack, and headed on home like all was normal. But everything wasn't normal and it was a miracle that I made it through that chase without any injuries. What started out to be a simple walk home turned into a run for my life.

I never knew just how fast and agile I was until that day.

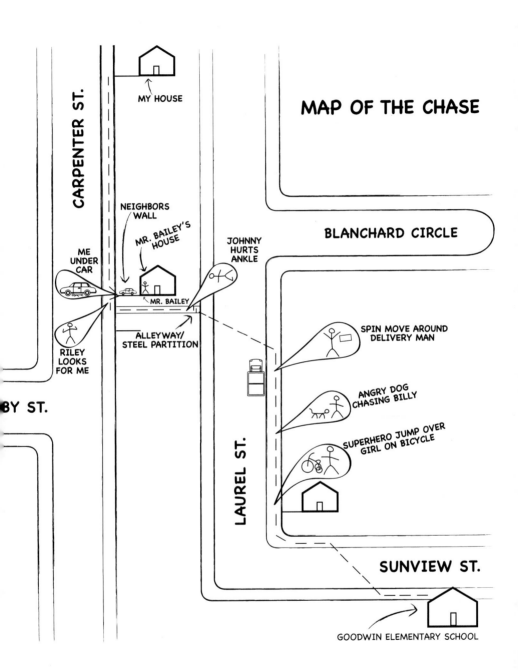

CHAPTER 11

YOU WANT A PARTY?

The day had come and gone and I was both happy and sad it was over. The Dilbonary, which was the only thing that I truly called my own, had been discovered. Riley and his band of no-gooders tried twice to take it from me, but I was able to keep it from them. However, I suspected that my luck wouldn't last too long.

It was almost time for dinner as Mother was preparing the food while Father and I occupied the living room. Father was looking through the mail and newspaper while I finished up my homework that I didn't do after school, on account of getting chased and almost getting run over by Mr. Bailey's car.

My mother had just finished putting the final touches on her meal and called us in for dinner. Father and I took our designated places at the dinner table. Mother followed in with her plates of food and displayed them in front of us. Mother loved to cook and she was good at it. She was proud of her meals as she could cook about anything and cook it well. There were only a few things she makes that absolutely disgusted me and she knew it. It just so happened that our dinner that night included one of those things.

The conversation between the two of them was always short, and so I became the talk of the table, as usual.

"So did you have a good day at school today, Dilby?" Mother asked, unaware of the day's events.

"Ah-huh," I said as I stuffed a pile of mashed potatoes in my mouth, trying to avoid talking.

"Anything exciting happen?" Father asked as he cut into his chunk of steak.

"Nope," I said as I avoided eye contact with them and focused on eating. The quicker I could finish dinner, the fewer questions I would have to answer. But I knew this would be a long dinner as I stared down at the squash on my plate that was getting colder by the second. I hated squash! There was nothing good about it. I told my parents every time that I didn't like it, but they still made me eat it.

I pushed the disgusting vegetable aside and continued scarfing down my meat and potatoes.

"So, Dilby, your birthday is coming up in a few days, the big eleven," Father said excitedly. "You haven't told us where you want to go for your birthday dinner yet."

I stopped eating, took a drink of my juice, and looked up to them.

"Actually, I was thinking about having a bitpog this year, if that's okay," I said.

"What's a bitpog?" Father asked.

"It's a party," I said. "I think I want to have one this year and invite some kids."

"A party!" Mother and Father said almost simultaneously, both shocked and surprised.

"You want a party?" Father said.

"Yeah, I think it'll be fun," I said. "But just a few kids, nothing big or anything."

"That's great sweetie," Mother said. "We'd love to have a bitpog for you."

"Well, that's quite the pawgull turn of events now, isn't it? Did I say that right, pawgull? Father said.

"Yeah," I said with a laugh.

"We're just a little surprised, that's all," Father said. "You've just never wanted a party before."

"Well, things changed," I said. "I've changed."

"Okay then, a party it is," Father said with a smile.

"Any particular type of bitpog you want?" Mother asked.

"Not really," I said. "Whatever is fine. You choose."

Mother and Father glowed with happiness. I think they were more excited than I was about this. They sat there bouncing ideas off one another, probably the most I ever heard them say to each other at the table. I continued eating as I piled my squash on one side of the plate, clearly showing my dismay for the vegetable.

"You know you still have to eat that," Mother said.

"Why? You know I hate squash," I said in a little whiny voice hoping for once they would say I wouldn't have to eat it. "It's gross."

"Then I guess you can't have any carrot cake that I made," Mother said.

Mother always knew how to get me to eat things I didn't like. Carrot cake was my most favorite dessert and I'd eat just about anything to have some of it.

"Fine, I'll eat it," I said, pouting like a baby. "But I want a big piece!"

A while later, after I had stuffed my face with carrot cake, which was so youpp, it was time for bed. I was exhausted from the day I had and couldn't wait to sleep it away.

I brushed my teeth, followed up by a **SWIGGLE**⋆ of bubble gum mouthwash and then hopped into my bouncy bed and pulled the cozy, comfy blankets over my skinny body. Before I closed my eyes, I rolled over and looked out my bedside window and stared out at the smooneys. I gripped the key around my neck with a fist and held it tight, hoping that my wish would soon come true.

As I lay waiting and watching in the dark, I thought about many things. Things like what would happen tomorrow at school or what I wanted for my birthday and what I might dream of that night. Where I would go, who I would be. My mind was racing with all kinds of thoughts.

Looking out at the smooneys, my eyes began to slowly close and eventually I fell into a deep sleep.

I needed something to inspire me so that I would be able to rise up and overcome great challenges. As I slept that night, I was about to find the inspiration I so desperately wanted. I dreamed the biggest dream I ever had, showing me that even though you're different, you can still be brave.

CHAPTER 12

ZOOMINS VS. PENTAKERS

"Fee-Fi-Fo-Fum, I smell the blood of a **WIKKE*** man!" I heard a girl's voice say as my eyes fluttered, not fully awake yet.

"I said, Fee-Fi-Fo-Fum, I smell the blood of a wikke man!" the same girl's voice yelled out.

As I opened my eyes, I saw a very tiny girl standing right in front of my face.

"Mornin' Dilby!" the tiny girl said as she tapped me on the nose. "Whatcha doin' over here?"

I sat up, rubbed my eyes, and took a big yawn and stretch. I looked around and noticed that I was in the middle of a forest. It all seemed normal except that everything around me looked smaller than it should be. The trees, the sky, the animals, the girl, they all looked miniature compared to me. It quickly became clear to me that I was not of normal size. In fact, I was a giant.

"You alright, Dilby?" the tiny girl said. "You never come this close to us."

I bent down to get a closer look at this girl. There was nothing odd about her, except she was about 100 times smaller than I was and wore even baggier clothes than I did.

"Close to who?" I said. "Where am I?"

It was clear that she knew me but I couldn't remember her. However, there was something familiar about this girl, only I couldn't seem to put my finger on where I knew her from. And then it hit me: the girl was a tiny version of my school teacher, Mrs. Weaver!

"That's a good one, Dilby," the tiny girl said as she laughed.

I had no idea what she was laughing about, but I knew she was laughing at me. I reached out my oversized arm and wrapped my huge hands around her, closing my thick fingers so she couldn't get away.

"What's so funny, Mrs. Weaver?" I said in a not-so-nice tone.

"What? No, Dilby. It's me, Simone!" the tiny girl said.

"You changed your name?" I asked.

"What do you mean?" the tiny girl said.

As I stood up on my feet, still holding on to Simone, I noticed that I was nearly as tall as the trees. I was dressed in tattered clothes that were just a little small but still covered my body. I had on worn-out sandals tied with leather straps that wrapped around my legs up to my knees. My body was big and strong and my hands were worn and rough.

"What is this place?" I asked.

"You're in Firr Briar Forest, land of Zoomin," Simone said. "And you, of course, are Dilby, but everyone calls you wikke."

"Wikke?" I asked. "Why wikke?"

"Well, that's who you are," Simone said proudly. "You're the giant, so that's what we call you."

"So, I'm the wikke," I said. "Why aren't you afraid of me then?"

"Well, you and me are **NOOK NOOKS***," Simone said.

"What in the world are nook nooks?" I asked with a puzzled look on my face.

"We are, you big silly! Only I'm not supposed to be nook nooks with you because Zoomins think you eat Zoomins, but really you don't, but they don't believe that because you're a wikke and everyone says don't trust a wikke because..." Simone rambled on and on, talking a hundred miles an hour.

"Wait, wait, wait, slow down. What the heck are Zoomins?" I asked.

"Well, I'm a Zoomin, you big goof," Simone said. "That's what my people are called."

I brought Simone right up to my mouth.

"So am I supposed to eat you?" I said.

I could see Simone was a little puzzled and unsure of what I would do. To be honest, I wasn't even sure of what I was supposed to do.

"NO! Dilby, you don't eat Zoomins!" Simone shouted.

"Mmmm, but you do look pretty tasty, Mrs. Weaver!" I said as I licked my lips with my big tongue. "And I sure am hungry!"

"That...that's not funny! And my name's not Mrs. Weaver," Simone said.

"There's not much to you so I would need to eat about a hundred of you to get full," I said. "So where are the rest of your people?"

"You don't want to do that! I'm...I'm not tasty!" Simone said as she struggled to break free from my grasp, but couldn't. "Now stop this, Dilby!"

I looked Simone up and down and licked my lips again. I opened my mouth up wide and brought her closer to my mouth.

"DILBY, STOOOPP!" Simone screamed out.

"Gotcha!" I said as I closed my mouth and let out a smile.

"That wasn't funny, Dilby," Simone said, relieved it was just a joke.

I may not have known who I was or who Simone was, even though she looked like Mrs. Weaver, or even where I was, but I did know that eating people was something that I would never do. Simone seemed like a nice girl and apparently we were nook nooks in this place, so I just went along with what she was telling me while I tried to figure things out.

"You should've seen your face, Simone!" I said, laughing. "Now that was funny!"

"Well, you should have seen your face," Simone said. "You had this weird look in your eyes and your tongue came all out at me, which, by the way, was pretty gross!"

"So did you really think I was gonna eat you?" I said.

"NO! Maybe...I don't know," Simone said, looking a little embarrassed.

"Now that would have been gross," I said.

"Eeeewwwww," Simone said as we both laughed.

Just then, a loud horn sounded off in the distance. It had a deep sounding tone as if someone was blowing through a metal tube.

Baaawwwwaaaa! Baaawwwwaaaa! Baaawwwwaaaa!

"That's the warning sound," Simone said. "Come on Dilby, we've got to go!"

I had no idea what was going on, but if that was a warning sound then that only meant something bad was going to happen. Bad things are what I always tried to avoid and what scared me. I wasn't a jinbone or a spinhoot or a fighter or someone who wished to do harm to anyone. This wasn't my problem and in no way did I want to get involved.

"I can't go with you little girl, sorry," I said as I set Simone back on the ground and walked the other way.

"Where you going, Dilby?" Simone shouted.

"I'm hungry," I said. "And since I can't eat you, I'm going to go find some food."

Simone ran up and stopped in front of me.

"Dilby, you have to help us!" Simone pleaded to me.

"No, I don't," I said matter of factly.

"I thought you were my nook nook!" Simone said. "Nook nooks help each other! That's my family, my people down there, and they need your help!"

"And what do you expect me to do?" I said.

"Fight for us!" Simone yelled. "Dilby, you're a wikke, you're not afraid of anyone. We need your help, please!"

Was Simone right? Was I not afraid of anyone? After all, I was a wikke, and who could hurt a wikke? This could be my moment, my time to prove to myself that I wasn't afraid any more, to be brave and stand up and fight. I was a wikke and no one was going to mess with me.

"Let's go fight some bad guys then!" I said as I scooped Simone back up into my hand and took off running toward the sounding siren.

The ground trembled with every big step I took, snapping trees in half as we rushed through the forest.

"That's far enough, Dilby, put me down," Simone yelled.

We stopped on top of the hill and I set Simone on the ground. We could see Firr Briar Village down at the bottom of the valley from where we were.

In the opposite direction, an army of soldiers was headed straight toward it.

"Look Dilby, Pentakers!" Simone said. "And they're about to attack Firr Briar!"

"Go help the others and find somewhere safe to hide," I said. "I'll fight them off and send them away!"

Without hesitating, I took off running and charged down the hill toward the Pentakers army, yanking two trees up on my way. Without thinking twice, I launched one of the trees in the air and it took off like a bullet, landing just in front of the attacking Pentakers before they reached Firr Briar. I couldn't believe the strength I had. I was launching 50-foot trees like they were pencils!

The army came to a quick halt. I could see that they had noticed me in the distance, as I stood holding up the other tree in the air like it was a sword.

"Fee-Fi-Fo-Fum, I smell the blood of army men!" I roared out as my voice echoed throughout the land for everyone to hear.

"It's the wikke!" the Pentaker General yelled out. "Archers, to your mount!"

A band of soldiers ran up to the front by the General and formed a solid line behind the big tree, guarding the General. The General then raised his arm in the air.

"Archers, on my order!" the General barked out.

The Archers loaded arrows into their bows and pulled back the strings, preparing to fire upon me.

"Let's put this wikke down!" the General shouted out.

The archers took aim at me.

"Fire!" the General yelled as he lowered his arm.

In an instant, the sky was filled with arrows as they rapidly cut through the air headed straight for me. I readied myself as I took the tree and started swinging it back and forth in front of me as the arrows rained down all around me.

I managed to knock most of the arrows away from me with the tree, but a few snuck by and hit me in the arms and legs. But the arrows didn't do any harm, they were like mosquito bites to a wikke like me, and the General and his army took notice of that.

Before the general was able to ready his gunmen, I took off in a full sprint, headed straight for the army with the tree still in my hands.

The general knew he didn't have to time to fire off his guns and if he stayed and tried to fight me it would be devastating to his army. So he did what any smart general would do.

"Retreat! Retreat!" the General yelled out his order.

The army quickly turned around and retreated as fast as they could, leaving behind a cloud of dust.

I dropped the tree and turned around facing the village. The Zoomin people had gathered in front of their village and were armed with weapons pointed at me. I guess they didn't know what to expect, because to them, I was still the wikke and they feared me.

From inside the crowd, Simone came running and stopped between me and her people.

"Everyone, put down your weapons. You can't hurt him with those! Besides, he's not going to hurt us!" Simone exclaimed. "Don't be scared, he's my nook nook."

"You can't be nook nooks with him, he's a wikke!" a man yelled out.

"He's going to eat us!" a woman exclaimed in fear.

The crowd erupted into a frenzy as I stood by and just laughed.

"He is not going to eat us!" Simone yelled out. "He doesn't eat Zoomins."

"And how do you know that, Simone?" another man asked.

"Because I've been his nook nook for a long time and look, he hasn't eaten me yet!" Simone said. "All the stories about this wikke, they're not true!"

For the first time in my life, someone was sticking up for me.

"Simone's right, I don't eat people," I said. "But I do like a tasty whale every now and then."

The crowd burst into a laugh.

"So fear me not, Zoomin people. I am your nook nook and I will protect you." I said.

I plucked one of the arrows out from my body, as though it was like a little thorn and held it up.

"And it's gonna take a lot more than this tiny arrow to hurt me," I said. "I'm the wikke, nothing can hurt me!"

The crowd roared and began to chant, WIKKE! WIKKE! WIKKE! WIKKE! WIKKE!

CHAPTER 13

LOOK, IT'S GIDLADER!

The night had ended and I awoke from my sleep with a big stretch and a long yawn. The bright sun streaking through my bedroom window hit me in the face that early Friday morning. As I lay in bed staring up at the ceiling, a smile formed on my face as I remembered my dream of being a wikke. For the first time in my life, I had become a hero for doing something brave and it felt liberating!

As I shifted to get out of bed, I felt something pricking me in my left leg. Upon inspection, I saw a thorn-like object sticking out of my leg. I carefully pinched the object between my fingernails and pulled it out. As I looked closer at it, I realized it was the tip of a Pentakers broken arrow!

"No freakin' way!" I exclaimed in disbelief.

As I stared at the arrow, I thought about the first time I brought something back from a dream. First, there was the pink and blue cotton candy from the land of coupensents and now this, a Pentakers arrow from Firr Briar. "This is so awesome," I said to myself.

This was truly amazing but I still couldn't understand how it all worked, being able to travel through time and to different worlds and then to bring stuff back. No matter how hard I tried to think about it, there was no logical explanation I could come up with for why this was happening to me.

As I sat at the breakfast table eating my soggy cereal, the thought of facing Riley and the other kids at school made my stomach a little nervous. I wanted to avoid school that day and the idea of faking being sick sounded pretty good to me.

I then recounted my dream of being a wikke and that nothing can hurt a wikke! If I could stand up to an entire army, why couldn't I stand up against one jinbone? This made me a lot less nervous and even gave me a little courage and confidence.

Now, you would have thought that after everything that happened the day before, I would have left the Dilbonary at home. It would have been the smart and logical thing to do. But feeling courageous and knowing Grace would be by my side, I felt confident enough to bring it.

After my pep talk with myself, I grabbed my backpack with the Dilbonary inside and headed off to school.

As I arrived at school, I headed for the front doors where Mr. Foster stood guard and saw him retrieving something from his fanny pack.

"Hey, Mr. Foster," I said as I casually strolled up the steps to the doors like I owned the school or something.

"Hey there, Dilby," Mr. Foster said as he looked up.

Inside the school, the long hallway was filled with kids rushing to their classrooms. I walked through the crowd and all seemed normal. I didn't see Riley and his band of no-gooders yet as kids were laughing and playing and doing what they usually do every morning. Maybe everyone didn't care or forgot about the Dilbonary and I worried for nothing. If no one had said anything to me by that point, there was a good chance no one would say anything at all. I could be home free.

I walked through the hallway with confidence now. My head was no longer down, avoiding the stares of other kids as I normally did. Instead, I said, "what's up" and "hey" to kids I normally wouldn't speak to. Of course, there were no responses but I didn't expect there to be. Nobody was even really paying attention to me, but that was nothing new, and that was a good sign.

As I got farther down the hallway and closer to my classroom, I started to notice changes in the way kids were acting. First, they started looking at me and watching me as I walked by them. Then came the whispering, followed by pointing and laughing.

And there it was: yet again, I was the joke.

Up ahead I saw Riley and his band of no-gooders, Johnny and Billy, leaning against the wall. They were watching me with their silly smirks on their faces as I walked through the hallway of shame toward them. I could tell they were waiting for me to arrive so they could begin to have their fun with me.

The confidence I once had when I walked past Mr. Foster had quickly run away, something I thought of doing myself, but I didn't. If Riley and the no-gooders didn't get me then, they would get me later and it would probably be worse.

As I made my way toward them, I had to show them that all the pointing and laughing that was directed at me didn't bother me or that I didn't care. So I kept my head up and ignored the humiliating whispers and remarks coming from all of the kids that I passed by.

I guess Riley didn't like that I wasn't reacting to everyone the way he thought I would, because what he did next changed everything.

Riley pushed away from the wall and walked over and stood in the middle of the hallway. The other kids made a clear path between Riley and me. I stopped and just stared him down. The hallway suddenly got quiet. I knew everyone was looking at me but I couldn't see them. It was like I had tunnel vision and all I could see was Riley at the other end of the hall staring me down like a bull ready to charge me.

I swallowed hard as my heartbeat rapidly increased. It felt like my heart was going to burst through my chest. I wiped my sweaty palms on my jeans. This was it; the time had come to battle. I was cornered, nowhere for me to run to. I was going to have to stand my ground and be the wikke I knew I could be.

Dilby vs. Riley! Ding, Ding, Ding!

Riley lifted his hand and pointed at me. "Hey everyone, look, it's the gidlader," he called out.

The whole hallway erupted in laughter, pointing, and chanting.

Gidlader! Gidlader! Gidlader! Gidlader! Gidlader!

I knew what I had coming would be bad, but I didn't expect that. That was just truly mean and embarrassing. The scene was like in a movie when everything goes into slow motion but you're still in normal speed. The people's faces get pawgull looking and the words make a deep sound and take forever to say.

Giiiiiiiidllaaaadddddeerrrrrr!

If only I was able to make time stand still or be invisible at that moment, I would have avoided facing what stood all around me, but I couldn't. When my mind stopped playing everything in slow motion and the noise settled down, Riley and his band of no-gooders had made their way to me.

"Hey there, gidlader!" Riley said with a demented giggle. "You like your new name, gidlader?"

Riley and the no-gooders continued to laugh.

"Yeah gidlader, how ya like it?" Johnny said.

I just stood there looking back at all of them, unsure of what to say or do. So I just blurted out the first thing that came to me.

"It's cool, I guess," I said.

"Cool? It's not cool, it's stupid," Riley said.

"Yeah, it's stupid," Billy said.

"It's kinda like that book of yours, what's it called... Dilbonary?" Riley said bobbing his head, proud that he pronounced it correctly, as everyone laughed. "So let's have it!"

"Have what?" I replied.

"The book, stupid. Give it to me!" Riley demanded.

I figured I had two choices. One, I could just cower down and give him the Dilbonary knowing I would never get it back while enduring even more never-ending humiliation. Or two, I could be the wikke and stand up to the jinbone.

"No," I said strongly as I looked him straight in the eyes.

"What did you say?" Riley said, as he got right up to my face.

"It's not yours," I said. "You can't have it."

"Last chance, gidlader," Riley said.

I just stood there silent and steadfast, standing my ground.

I prepared myself for whatever Riley was going to do. If he wanted the Dilbonary he would have to take it from me. I gripped my backpack tight. The tension was building for something to happen. The hallway was void of noise as the kids looked on with anticipation. Then…I dropped to the floor on one knee and clutched my stomach. Riley's punch to my gut was too fast for me to see coming and it buckled me.

As I remained hunched over on the floor, my backpack became exposed and faced Riley. I tried to fight him off as he grabbed it, unzipped it and took out the Dilbonary. I finally got to my feet and tried to take it back from him but he just pushed me back down like I was nothing.

I looked up from the ground and spotted Grace standing in the crowd behind Riley. I could see the sadness in her eyes before she looked away, like she was disappointed in herself for not helping me.

The crowd was hooting and hollering as Riley held up the Dilbonary above his head for all to see. He paraded it like he had just won the jinbone championship belt.

I knelt there on the ground, humiliated. I knew I needed to do something and I needed to do it right then. Suddenly, I felt something come over me that I hadn't felt before. Deep anger was coursing its way through me and I felt a surge of strength. I rose to my feet, stood up straight and dropped my backpack to the ground. I looked at Riley with a dead stare as he still held up the Dilbonary, laughing. My breathing became more rapid and I started to shake uncontrollably as the adrenaline was pumping through my body. The fight wasn't over yet.

Then, in a flash, I became the wikke.

I charged at Riley, tackling him to the ground. The Dilbonary went flying out of his hands disappearing into the crowd of kids. I sat up on top of Riley looking down on him. I was so mad at Riley and wanted to hurt him, but I couldn't bring myself to hit him, so I just screamed in his face.

Fight, fight, fight!

Everyone around us began to chant. I was in shock of what I just did and I wasn't quite sure what to do next since I'd never been in a fight before. I could see Riley didn't like being in that position, and in one big move he threw me off of him and pounced on top of me. He was about to put a hurt on me when Mr. Foster pushed his way through the crowd and stopped it.

"Hey, hey, hey! Knock it off! Enough!" Mr. Foster yelled as he grabbed Riley and pulled him off of me.

"Everyone, get to your classes, now!" Mr. Foster yelled out as the crowd slowly dispersed.

"Except for you two, you stay!"

I got up from the ground and stood between Mr. Foster and Riley.

"Someone want to explain this?" Mr. Foster said with a stern tone.

"Gidlader started it," Riley said, all innocent like as he looked at Mr. Foster.

"Who?" Mr. Foster asked.

"Him," Riley said, pointing to me. "He tackled me first!"

"Because you punched me and stole my journal," I said.

"Is that true?" Mr. Foster asked Riley. "You punched him?"

"No!" Riley said.

"Liar," I replied.

"You're a liar," Riley fired back.

"Enough!" Mr. Foster said. "I should send you both to the principal's office for this. But I'm not going to do that. Instead, you're going to shake hands and apologize to each other for this nonsense."

"Not until he gives me back my journal," I said.

"What journal?" Mr. Foster asked.

"I don't have your stupid book," Riley said.

"Then where is it?" I said.

"Riley, do you have his book?" Mr. Foster asked.

"It's a journal!" I said.

"Book, journal, whatever it is. Do you have it or not?" Mr. Foster asked.

"No, I don't have his book," Riley said.

"He said he doesn't have it, Dilby," Mr. Foster said.

"He's lying!" I said. "He took it from my backpack and showed everyone."

"What is this book anyway?" Mr. Foster asked me.

"It's a journal. And it's nothing," I said.

"Well, if it's nothing then I guess it doesn't matter," Mr. Foster said.

I looked at Riley as he smirked back at me. If he didn't have the Dilbonary, then someone in the crowd must have took it. Maybe the no-gooders have it. If so, it would surely get to Riley and I would never get it back.

The bell sounded for school to start.

"Now, shake hands and apologize," Mr. Foster said.

Why did I have to apologize? It should have been Riley saying sorry. I didn't do anything wrong. But if it meant avoiding the principal's office, then fine, I'd suck it up.

I extended my hand out to Riley who gave me more of a slap than a shake as we said sorry.

"Good. Now I don't want to catch you two going at it again, otherwise there will be serious consequences," Mr. Foster said. "You understand?"

Riley and I looked away from each other keeping silent.

"Do you understand?" Mr. Foster said in an elevated voice.

"Yes," I said.

"Yeah," Riley responded.

"You're late, so get to class," Mr. Foster said.

I grabbed my backpack from the ground and headed off to class as I followed Riley keeping my distance from him. Riley reached the classroom and opened the door. Before he went in, he looked back at me as I approached the door.

"You're not going to escape me today, gidlader!" Riley said quietly in a threatening tone. "When school gets out, you're as good as dead!"

CHAPTER 14

A TASTE OF HIS OWN MEDICINE

I wasn't sure what kind of day I was going to have when I entered the school, but after my showdown with Riley in the hallway and his threatening remark, I knew it was probably going to be bad.

After the first three hours in class, all was quiet on the home front between Riley and I. At the square table he hadn't spoken one word to me or even glanced in my direction. I wasn't sure if I was relieved by that or scared. In fact, everyone treated me like I was invisible. Even worse, I still didn't know who had the Dilbonary, but I figured it would get in the hands of Riley at lunch if the no-gooders had it.

After debating how I should handle the rest of the day, I decided to face the monster head on again at lunchtime and try to get the Dilbonary back if he had it.

As I entered the cafeteria with my lunch, I was hoping to not sit alone as I scanned the room looking for Grace. Since showing Grace the Dilbonary, we had become nook nooks. I trusted her and she believed in me, which made us perfect nook nooks, at least that's how I looked at it. But I was surprised when she didn't help me in the hallway with Riley early that morning, which made me question our friendship. I had to find out the truth.

I spotted Grace sitting at a table by herself near the back so I made a beeline straight for her. I didn't see Riley and no-gooders in the cafeteria but I hurried anyway and plopped down in a seat across from Grace. She looked up at me and then looked around, almost surprised to see me. She seemed nervous or uncomfortable with my presence and she just put her head down and continued eating her lunch.

The silence between us was making it very awkward, so I decided to break it.

"Someone got your tongue?" I said.

Grace remained head down.

"I thought we were nook nooks?" I said.

That prompted Grace to look up at me.

"What?" she said, clearly not knowing what nook nooks meant.

"I showed you the Dilbonary. I trusted you," I said.

Grace looked around then slightly lifted up her food tray and slid the Dilbonary that was underneath it over to me. My eyes widened in shock and disbelief as I quickly grabbed it and slid it underneath me, sitting on it.

"How did you get this?" I whispered.

"I grabbed it from the floor when Riley dropped it," Grace said quietly.

"I've been going kweek this whole time thinking Johnny or Billy had it and they were going to give it to Riley." I said. "Thank you, Grace, for holding on to it for me and keeping it safe. You have no idea how happy I am to have it back."

"You're welcome," Grace said with a smile.

Then, in an instant, her face and demeanor turned to sadness and regret.

"I'm sorry, Dilby, but I can't talk to you right now," Grace said.

I could tell she was ashamed to say that.

"Why?" I asked.

"I'm already Brace Face Grace and I don't need another bad name. I just wanted to give you back the Dilbonary because it's yours," Grace said.

I was confused at first why she had said that. And then it became clear as to why she was acting that way toward me. Grace had been exposed to the Riley virus.

"I'm sorry," Grace said as she put her head back down to her lunch.

It's hard being a pawgull kid in school and I certainly didn't want to be the cause of someone getting made fun of. Besides, she saved the Dilbonary for me and gave it back. Maybe she still was my nook nook, but I didn't know for sure. So I just let it go and pretended we were strangers once again.

I opened my lunch bag and took out my ham sandwich and chips and began to eat. I tried not to think about Grace but it was hard, knowing she was sitting right across from me.

Now that I had the Dilbonary back I didn't need to confront Riley anymore. As my eyes floated around the room I saw Riley and the no-gooders eating on the other side of the cafeteria. They were laughing and messing around, no doubt up to no good.

I looked away to avoid being seen by them and settled on a corner of a wall behind Grace. I stopped eating and just stared at the brick wall. Then, I began to drift off into a daydream of my own world.

First came the silence, then the darkness.

When I opened my eyes, I was standing on top of a barren hill overlooking a huge desert plain. It had mountains and valleys in it with big boulders and tons of shrubs and small trees scattered around. There was even a river flowing through it that branched off in several different directions. The place was peaceful and beautiful, as though it had never been touched by any human.

As breathtaking as it was, there was more than meets the eye to that place. When I finally got over the initial sight of the desert plain, I started noticing **FURWATTNIDS*** all around the land.

There weren't just a few; it was an army of all different kinds of furwattnids roaming around for as far as I could see. For a moment, I thought I was in a nightmare when a family of skunks came walking up to me. I froze hoping to not be sprayed in that horrible smell, not to mention I had a severe allergy that prevented me from being around any furwattnids, particularly ones with fur. I loved furwattnids but any contact would send me into a severe allergic attack, which made me sneeze and wheeze.

After a short time of being around them, I realized that I was fine. I had no allergic reactions and I wasn't sprayed with skunk odor, either. They were brushing up against my legs and acting like pets around me.

"If I didn't have any reaction to the skunks, maybe I won't with any of the other furwattnids," I thought to myself.

So without thinking twice, I ran down the hill toward the furwattnids and I noticed that they were watching me coming at them. Instead of running away like they normally would, they either approached me or stayed where they were. It seemed I was in no danger from them or allergic to them as I ventured through the valley into the sea of furwattnids.

There was every type of furwattnid I could think of from small to big, skinny to fat, and short to tall. They were all friendly and just as curious about me as I was about them.

"This place is incredible," I thought. It was better than any zoo imaginable.

After what seemed like hours and hours of embracing the Land of Furwattnids, that's what I named it, I was fizzy dizzy and slappy happy from playing with all of them.

Somehow I found myself huddled up with a lion on top of some large flat boulders under a huge shade tree that perched out above the desert. The lion calmly sat next me as I ran my hand through his soft fur, petting him as you would a dog.

I could hear him purring as I stroked my hand down his back. I felt safe with him there and I took that as a sign of his acceptance of me. It's hard to describe the feeling I had as the lion and I just hung out enjoying each other's company as we watched herds of giraffes and zebras and elephants and all other furwattnids graze on by, like we were two old nook nooks watching a football game or something. There was nothing that could ruin that moment. It was perfect.

And then...the unpredictable, the unthinkable, the unimaginable happened.

As I lay nestled peacefully next to the lion, I heard the most horrible voice coming from behind me.

"GIDLADER, WHERE AM I?" the voice screeched out.

My heart jumped and I cringed at the sound of that. It was like hearing nails on a chalkboard.

"No way. It can't be," I said to myself.

I quickly turned around and saw Riley standing behind me in the distance in the boulders. We locked eyes, both in complete shock and surprise.

"How on earth did Riley get in my dream?" I thought.

"What is this?" Riley said looking confused and scared. "What's going on, gidlader?"

I've never seen this side of Riley. He was actually scared, especially when the lion stood up and roared at him.

"That's...that's a lion, gidlader!" Riley exclaimed. "Why is he staring at me that way?"

The lion stood in front of me like he was protecting me. The lion was staring Riley down like he was a tasty morsel.

"I guess he doesn't like you, Riley," I said. "And if I were you, I wouldn't make any sudden moves."

"Just keep him back, gidlader!" Riley said, like he was giving me an order.

In that instant, I lost it.

"OR WHAT, RILEY?" I said in an angry tone. "I'm tired of being pushed around by you! What did I ever do to you that made you treat me so badly?"

For the first time in my life, I stood up for myself, and to Riley of all people. I guess I had had enough of his jinboning because I had never felt that mad in my life. Riley was silent and surely was taken aback by my reaction. He had no answer or comeback for my question, which was a first.

I walked up close to Riley as the lion walked with me by my side. I could see this made Riley scared and nervous as he took a few steps back, but I didn't care. I kind of liked that it made him uneasy.

"You're just a mean kid, Riley...you're just mean," I said.

"Yeah, well just you're a loser, gidlader!" Riley said as he moved forward at me with a raised voice. "And that stupid book of yours, it ain't gonna make you cool."

ROOOOAAARRRRRR!

Riley stumbled back, almost falling to the ground. It was clear from the roar that the lion did not like Riley or the way he spoke to me. I wanted to be mad at what Riley said but there was a bigger problem going on than just Riley's words.

"How did you get here Riley?" I asked.

"I don't know," Riley replied.

"Well, what's the last thing you remember?" I said.

"What are you talking about?" Riley blurted out.

"Before I came here, I was sitting down across from Grace at lunch in the cafeteria," I said trying to remember the events. "Everything was normal and then somehow you're here. So something must of happened."

"Nothing happened," Riley yelled back.

I didn't believe him and neither did the lion as the lion let out another big roar!

"Clearly something happened, Riley!" I said in a raised voice.

"Okay! Yeah, I went up to you and asked you a question but you didn't answer. You just sat there looking at the wall," Riley blurted out.

I wasn't convinced that was all that happened and it was clear he had more to say as he looked away from me and got really quiet.

"And then what?" I asked. "Tell me, Riley, what did you do?"

"You were ignoring me so I grabbed you, so what?" Riley said.

"That's it!" I said. "That's gotta be why you're here. When you grabbed me you must've somehow brought yourself into my dream."

"Huh?" Riley said. "Now you're just talking stupid, gidlader!"

"Look around us, Riley," I said with my arms wide open. "Does this look like the cafeteria?"

Just then, furwattnids of all kinds came out of nowhere and surrounded us, forming a circle. It was as though I had summoned them there to come protect me, but I didn't. Riley took notice of them and saw that he was surrounded and trapped.

"What is this?" Riley said with fear in his voice.

I slowly spun around and looked at all the furwattnids and the massive land that we were standing in.

"This is my dream, all of this!" I said. "Only thing is, my dreams...they're real."

Riley let out a sarcastic laugh as a silly smirk appeared on his face.

"Real? And you wonder why you have no friends." Riley said. "You're just a scared, weird kid with a stupid book!"

"Yeah, maybe. But we're in my world now." I said. "And in here, you're the one who should be scared."

"I'm not scared of anything, gidlader, especially you!" Riley yelled out, pointing his finger at me.

"Well, you should be, because you're not the big, bad jinbone here," I said sarcastically as the circle of furwattnids started to close in on Riley. "Have fun!"

As I turned and began to walk away, I could hear the fear in Riley's voice as he yelled out, "HEY! HEY, WHERE YOU GOING?"

When I turned back to answer him, I could see that a skunk was right behind him.

"I wouldn't turn around if I were you," I yelled back.

Of course Riley turned around and PSSHHHHHHHHH, the skunk sprayed him right in the face.

"AAAAHHHHHHHHHHHH!" Riley screamed and jumped around, trying to wipe off the skunk spray.

"I told you not to turn around," I said, laughing.

"That isn't funny!" Riley said, gagging and coughing as he spit out some skunk spray that had gotten in his mouth.

"Well, neither is punching me and taking the Dilbonary then making fun of me, but you did it anyway," I said.

"Ahh, this is so gross!" Riley said.

"Good!" I said.

"You're gonna pay for this, gidlader!" Riley yelled out.

"You like spiders, Riley, or snakes?" I asked.

"Why?" Riley asked.

"No reason, except they're about to crawl all over you," I said.

Riley looked down at the ground and saw a couple giant pythons slithering through his legs and a whole bunch of tarantula spiders crawling on his shoes.

"AHHHHHHHHH!" Riley screamed like a crying baby. "GET 'EM OFF ME! GET 'EM OFF ME!"

"I wouldn't move too fast. They can sense fear," I said, not knowing if that was true, but it sure sounded good. "Wait, I thought you weren't scared of anything, Riley."

"I'm not… I just don't like snakes or spiders," Riley said, trying so hard not to show his fear. "Now get 'em off me already!"

The tarantulas had slowly started to make their way up his legs.

"I think it's the skunk smell they like," I said. "You do smell pretty bad."

"Why are you doing this to me?" Riley said, whimpering.

"I'm not doing anything. You're the one who came into my dream," I said.

I wanted to help Riley but at the same time I wanted him to feel how he makes me feel when he and his band of no-good-ers mess with me. Honestly, I didn't really know how to help him. The furwattnids were acting on their own.

"Then how do I get out of here?" Riley said.

"Beats me," I said. "How about you try not being mean for once. All the furwattnids here get along with each other because they're not mean. I guess you just have to be nice."

"What in the world are furwattnids?" Riley asked.

"The animals, Riley, the ones that are crawling up your leg," I said. "Why don't you try thinking happy thoughts and acting nice, that's what I would do."

I hated helping Riley but I could see that he was vulnerable and I felt bad for him. He wasn't comfortable with being the victim, especially when he was asking for my help.

At first, Riley was stubborn and reluctant to take my advice. But as the tarantulas and pythons were inching up his body, he quickly understood that if he didn't listen to me, he would be covered in spiders and snakes, two things he was indeed afraid of.

Riley didn't have a choice and as much as he hated being told what to do, he closed his eyes and concentrated. I could only assume he was thinking happy thoughts because the next thing I remember was everything going silent and then black.

CHAPTER 15

THE SKUNKSTER IS BORN

The Land of Furwattnids had disappeared as the darkness that had come over me had slowly turned to light and I could begin to make out blurry figures in front of me. My hearing had quickly recovered as the faint sounds of laughter and chatter filled my ears.

Once I regained my vision, I could see that we were back inside the cafeteria. I was still sitting down at the table and Riley was standing next to me holding my arm. He quickly let go of me and started slapping at his body and jumping around like he was trying to swat something off him.

A small crowd of kids had gathered around us, including the no-gooders. They all had their noses plugged with their fingers and were shaking their heads because Riley smelled like a skunk. I looked up at Riley who still looked freaked out by what had just happened.

"It's not very fun is it? Being laughed at," I said to Riley.

"What just happened?" Riley said to me, tight lipped and looking very confused.

"I guess you learned how it feels to be me," I said. "And if I'm still the gidlader, then that makes you the skunkster!"

I waved my hand in front of my nose as everyone began laughing, even the no-gooders. That was the first time I had seen Riley get embarrassed. He wasn't quite sure how to handle himself as he stood there realizing that he was the butt of the joke instead of someone else.

"What are you all laughing at?" Riley yelled as he looked around at everyone.

"You, Riley," Grace said from behind me.

Riley cracked a sarcastic smirk and shook his head at Grace.

"You think this is sooo funny, don't you?" Riley said as he looked at me.

Riley grabbed me by the shoulder and I could see the anger in his eyes.

"I don't know what you just did to me, but I'm nothing like you, gidlader," Riley said. "This isn't over."

"If you say so, skunkster," I replied, and the crowd laughed once again.

Riley let go of me, then took off through the crowd as they backed away from his stinky body, making a path for him to pass.

The no-gooders chased after Riley with their noses plugged as the crowd dispersed.

Riley would never admit it, but he knew he deserved everything that happened to him. We all saw something in him that day that he never showed before. He might act tough to everyone, but deep down, he was afraid just like the rest of us.

After I watched Riley leave the cafeteria, I turned around in my seat to face Grace.

"So...what happened in there?" Grace asked eagerly.

"Not sure really. Maybe everything, maybe nothing," I said.

Grace tilted her head not really knowing what that meant.

"Either way, that was so awesome, what you did to Riley," Grace said with a big smile.

"What exactly did I do to Riley?" I asked.

"What do you mean?" Grace asked. "You don't know?"

"Just that he walked up and grabbed me," I said.

"Yeah, and then you told him he's a big jinbone jerk and you're not going to be afraid of him anymore and neither is anyone else," Grace exclaimed. "And what's a jinbone?"

"A bully. And then what happened?" I said.

"Riley started dancing around like he was on fire or something and then he started smelling like a skunk," Grace said. "And that's when we all started laughing at him."

"And that's it?" I asked.

"Yeah, pretty much," Grace replied.

That was the moment I realized that the time in real life is only a fraction of the time that is spent in my time dreams. Time as we know it slows way down in reality to mere seconds when in your dreams it feels like hours have gone by. This was truly mind blowing.

"I'm sorry Dilby, for acting like a jerk earlier," Grace said apologetically. "We're still friends?"

I wanted to be mad at Grace and tell her no, but I just couldn't do it. After all, I liked her...I liked her a lot.

"Nook nooks," I said with a smile.

She looked at me with a puzzled look.

"It means friends," I said.

"Nook nooks...I like it," she said as she smiled back acknowledging my forgiveness.

"You have something on you," Grace said as she pointed at my chest.

I looked down on my shirt and saw that there was a small clump of hair attached to it. I pulled it off and looked at it. It was the brown hair from the lion mane.

"What is it?" Grace asked.

I rubbed the soft hair between my fingers as I remembered the lion and what it did for me.

"It's courage," I said with a thoughtful smile.

Grace and I sat together for the remainder of lunch as she quizzed me about the world Riley and I visited. The fact that she loved furwattnids made it even better and she hung on every word of the story.

There was something about Grace that drew me to her. It wasn't the fact that she was talking to me or that we were nook nooks, it was more than that. She was genuinely fascinated by what I had to say about the Dilbonary and the worlds I had visited. For the first time in my short life, somebody my age got me. With all my quirks, Grace actually liked me for person I was.

I wasn't scared anymore to reveal my innermost secrets to her and after school I told her everything. She was so excited about my stories and adventures that she begged to be part of them. Next time I time dreamed, she wanted to go with me like Riley had.

I explained to her that I didn't know how it all worked; that Riley might have simply been an accident and that I wasn't sure if it could even happen again.

"Maybe it's as simple as me touching you," she said.

"Maybe, but I'm not sure," I said.

"Well, maybe we should try it and see what happens," she said anxiously.

I didn't feel comfortable about it, messing with the unknown, especially when it involved someone other than me.

"I don't even know what all this is or even how it works," I said. "I just think it's a bad idea, at least for now. Okay?"

She accepted that answer but made me promise that if I ever figured out how I could safely bring people into my time dream that she would be the first person I would take. Promise or no promise, I would have chosen her first anyway because she believed in me when I needed her to.

"One more thing, Grace," I said. "If you ever see me dreaming, you have to swear you won't touch me, at least until I figure this thing out, okay?"

Grace just sat silently, looking at me with big, sad puppy dog eyes. She didn't want to make that promise. Her curiosity and excitement was getting the best of her.

"Swear, Grace," I said.

She let out a deep sigh.

"Okay, I won't." Grace said.

I looked at Grace unsatisfied with her answer and she knew it. I needed to her say the words.

"Fine, I swear," Grace said. "Cross my heart and hope to die, stick a needle in my eye."

We both smiled, trusting each other's word. All I needed to do now was try to figure it out, to learn more about these time dreams before I attempted to bring Grace into one.

CHAPTER 16

IT'S GOOD TO BE THE HUDDLEMUGGER

It was Saturday, the day after the Riley encounter in the Land of Furwattnids. It was also the day of my 11th birthday and it was time for my bitpog.

It was 11:11 in the morning according to my watch when I had looked at it again for the umpteenth time and no one had arrived to my bitpog, which was supposed to start at 11 o'clock. I was sitting all alone at the patio table in my backyard with my head resting on the palm of my hand, just looking down at the table and fidgeting with a plastic fork.

I had surely thought things had changed for the better after what had happened in the cafeteria between Riley and me. Not only that, I ended up showing a bunch of kids the Dilbonary after school that day, a decision I reached at Grace's suggestion. I was scared at the thought of revealing it, the one thing I had kept secret for so long. It was hard showing Grace, but to put it out there for the whole school to see, that's an entirely new game that I wasn't sure I wanted to play.

The more Grace talked about how cool the Dilbonary was and that the other kids would think the same way, she was slowly convincing me to show it off.

Initially I had only invited two people to the bitpog, Grace and Harold, because, well, they were the only two people that I thought might actually come. But as I showed the Dilbonary to everyone, they seemed to like it and to like me as well. So I blurted out an invite to my bitpog to all the kids that were there, even though I didn't even really know most of them. It sounded like a good idea when I said it, so why not? Surprisingly, a lot of them said they would come, which, of course, got me pretty excited.

Well, I guess that was just way too much to hope for. At the very least, I would have bet on Grace being there since we were nook nooks again, but she was not. So there I sat, alone at the table feeling sad and sorry for myself. I had gotten all hyped up about having a great bitpog only to set myself up for disappointment.

I saw my parents looking out from the kitchen window probably feeling the same way for me. They had put a lot of time and effort into making a very festive time for me with all sorts of food and drinks, decorations, games, and even a giant star piñata. It had all the makings of a fantastic bitpog, except no one else was there to enjoy it.

As I sat there continuing to wallow in my self-pity, my mind began to drift and I began to do what I always do in times of boredom or crisis. Everything went quiet and my vision slowly started to fade out, eventually going to black.

DUH NAH NAH NAH, NAH NAH NAH...THUMP THUMP THUMP!

My eyes opened to a blue sky above me as I heard the sound of blazing horns and felt the ground tremble beneath me. I quickly sat up and turned around only to see a gaggle of men on horses dressed as knights in shining armor charging toward me.

As the knights approached me and stopped, they hopped off the horses and each knelt down on one knee before me as their armor banged and clanged.

"All hail, Sir Huddlemugger Dilby of Northerndale," the Knights exclaimed.

Surely they weren't talking to me. Confused, I looked to see who was behind me but no one was there. I turned back to the knights and soon realized they were indeed referring to me. I wasn't sure where I was, only that it was not Firr Briar and I wasn't a wikke. No, I was something bigger. I was a **HUDDLEMUGGER***!

The knights remained down on one knee until I decided to stand up. Once on my feet, the knight's rose and the head knight approached me and removed his helmet. To my shock, the head knight was Riley Rogers! His appearance was different and he spoke somewhat intelligently with an English accent, but it was Riley for sure.

"My huddlemugger, everyone in the city has been searching for you," said head knight Riley. "The **FAIREBLOSSOM***
has been in distress over your absence and requires your company by her side. You must come at once."

I had no idea what he was talking about. I was still trying to figure out how Riley was in my dream again. Only this time, he knew me as his huddlemugger and I knew him as my head knight.

"Sire, we must go," head knight Riley said with urgency.

Clearly this matter was of importance and time was a factor. After all, I was the huddlermugger and I was needed by my faireblossom.

"Then to the castle we go!" I shouted.

I hopped on a horse and followed the knights as we raced down a narrow tree-lined dirt road that went through the countryside. This was rather pawgull because I had never ridden a horse before, but in that place I rode like a champion!

After what seemed like hours on the horse, we finally reached Northerndale Castle. I've seen castles in books and movies but they were nothing like that one was. I had never seen a castle that big with its massive front walls and multiple towers. There were guards positioned all over and cannons stuck out of the ramparts.

The knights and I crossed over the wooden drawbridge that lowered down upon our arrival. The bridge extended over the moat and led to a massive steel gate that we entered through.

Once inside the castle walls, I hopped off my horse and was led into a building. I was rushed down a candle-lit hallway that led to two huge wooden doors at the end where a guard held a pillow with a golden-jeweled crown resting upon it. Once again, there was someone else I knew. The guard was Harold, who sat next to me in Mrs. Weaver's class.

"Your **QUIVTAR***, Huddlemugger Dilby," Harold the guard said, presenting it to me.

It was the coolest thing I'd ever seen. It was lined with diamonds and emeralds and rubies. I stared at it in awe for a moment then looked to Harold then back to the quivtar. I reached out my arms and hands and carefully took the quivtar from the pillow. It was much heavier than I thought it would be. I placed it atop my head and it fit perfectly. It felt all too familiar to me, like I had known what to do.

Then, from behind me someone came up and placed a big, heavy, red colored robe over me.

"Your **BUMBERNELL***, sire," a voice said.

As the person came around the front to adjust the bumbernell, I had noticed it was George. He finished tying the bumbernell, bowed to me, and then walked off.

With my bumbernell and quivtar on, I stood up tall and puffed out my chest, signs of a true huddlemugger! I then walked over and stood in front of the wooden doors where two guards stood by, one on each side. Upon a closer look, I realized the guards were Riley's band of no-gooders, Billy and Johnny. I guess they knew their place in the castle because they never made eye contact with me. I smiled knowing I was their huddlemugger and I raised my hand signaling them to open the doors and present me.

They opened the wooden doors and I stepped out onto a large balcony that overlooked an arena as horns blasted out. The arena was filled with thousands of people who cheered my arrival.

"My huddlemugger, you are here at last!" exclaimed Faireblossom Grace, who rushed over to me. "The games cannot start without you."

I was quite overwhelmed by what I saw. Faireblossom Grace was none other than Grace Billings. This Grace however, looked completely different. She had no braces and no glasses. Her hair was beautifully curled and her clothes were extravagant. She was the most beautiful girl I had ever seen and I couldn't take my eyes off her.

"Are you alright, my love?" Faireblossom Grace whispered in my ear.

Grace had called me her love! I blushed and giggled. No one had ever called me their love before. I looked out over the arena, taking in all that was mine. I had never felt more proud and confident or admired and popular as I did right then, standing there smiling the biggest smile I'd ever smiled.

"Never better, my faireblossom, never better," I said as I looked into her eyes "Come, let us start the games and take in this festive occasion together!"

I took Faireblossom Grace by her hand and led us to our thrones where we waved to the crowd of people, and together we signaled the start of the games. The games commenced as two chariots came rumbling into the arena and began to race around. Both chariots then stopped below the balcony and the riders got off and removed their helmets. The crowd cheered as the riders looked up at Faireblossom Grace and I and bowed to us.

It took me a second, but I soon realized who the riders were. On the left side was Donnie the spinhoot. He looked more muscular than normal and wore a leather outfit with a sword on his left hip.

On the right side was Mr. Foster. He, too, wore a leather outfit and sword and was just as muscular as Donnie. They placed their helmets back on, hopped on their chariots, and off they went to race each other.

Faireblossom Grace and I sat down on our thrones to enjoy the games. Three lovely maidens, who coincidentally happened to be the pop girls, Delia, Bella and Hailey, brought us food and drinks.

It was then that I figured out that Grace, along with Riley, Harold, George, Billy, Johnny, Donnie, Mr. Foster, Delia, Bella, and Hailey were there because I had created them in the dream. If they were there like Riley had been in the Land of Furwattnids, they would have been themselves and not someone else. They were clearly different which only meant that I had put them there and made them who I wanted them to be.

This was the life I had dreamed about, to simply be someone people acknowledged. I didn't need to be a huddlemugger, but since I was, I was going to enjoy every second of it. And best of all, I had Grace by my side, who I undoubtedly had a crush on.

I knew that I couldn't stay there forever and that the Northerndale world would be short lived, as I would eventually come out of my time dream. Even though no one was at my party back home, I still had my parents there to celebrate with, who I would miss forever if I couldn't return.

As I sat there on my throne thinking about that, the cheering crowd in the arena and all that was Northerndale slowly started to fade away and then went black.

The next thing I remember hearing was the sound of laughing and screaming voices. When I opened my eyes, I saw everyone I invited from school crowded around the table cheering for me. Grace was sitting next to me with a big smile on her face.

"Happy Birthday, King Dilby!" Grace said.

Everyone followed by yelling out happy birthday to me as they dove into the food and drinks and games. I truly was shocked and surprised by all this revelry because even though it was something I was not expecting, it was indeed the bitpog I always wanted. My parents stood to the side watching and smiling.

At first, I didn't know why Grace had decided to call me King Dilby, that was until I felt something resting on my head. When I reached up to grab it, I realized I was still wearing the quivtar from Northerndale.

But perhaps the biggest surprise of all was standing at the other end of the table. It was Riley and his band of no-gooders – one on each side of him. Riley and I just stared at each other for a moment, like we were in a gunfight waiting to see who would draw first. I wasn't quite sure why he had shown up, except to maybe wreck the party and get even with me for what happened yesterday.

And then, Riley drew first.

"Happy Birthday, gidlader," Riley said straight faced without any emotion attached to his words.

"Thanks, skunkster!" I said with a head nod back.

Clearly there was still tension between us and Grace watched intently to see what was going to happen next.

"We cool?" I said.

Riley took in a deep breath then exhaled as he made his way over to my side of the table and stood looking down at me. I wasn't sure what was about to happen, but I braced myself for whatever Riley was going to do to me.

"We're cool. But…" Riley leaned down to me and whispered, "I still want to know what you did to me and how you did it."

Riley stood back up as I looked him in the eyes.

"If we ever become nook nooks, maybe I'll tell ya," I said.

Riley cocked his head to one side and smirked at me, not knowing what nook nooks meant. He accepted the answer and signaled to the no-gooders as they ambled off toward the food table.

I looked at Grace and we just laughed a little. We both were shocked by Riley's behavior and how he was so forgiving after being humiliated the day before.

Right about then, George walked up and sat down next to me. It was clear he wanted to say something but was having a hard time getting it out.

"What's up George?" I asked.

He was nervous as he shoved a piece of gummy candy in his mouth. Grace and I looked at each other wondering about George. He finished chewing his candy and looked to me.

"It was me, I'm sorry," George said apologetically.

"For what?" I said.

"I told Riley about the Dilbonary," George said.

"But you told me it wasn't you," I said.

"I know, I lied, I'm sorry," George said showing remorse. "He saw us talking that morning and he threatened to stick my head in a toilet if I didn't tell him what we were talking about. So I told him."

"Well, at least now you know who told Riley," Grace said.

"I'm sorry Dilby," George said. "I didn't know Riley would do what he did."

I was mad at first when George told me, but the more I thought about it, my 6th grade life wouldn't have turned out the way it did if he never told Riley. And I probably never would have been nook nooks with Grace.

"It's okay, George," I said. "In a way, I have you to thank for all this happening," as I motioned to everyone at the bitpog.

"So you're not mad?" George said.

"How could I be?" I said. "I'm King Dilby!"

We all laughed and smiled and went about enjoying the bitpog.

That was truly one of the best days of my life! It certainly was the day that changed everything for me.

CHAPTER 17

REVELATIONS

My 11th birthday had turned out to be everything I wanted it to be. I never would've imagined in a million years that the Dilbonary would be the one thing that got kids to like me. Who would of thought that a pawgull kid who had pawgull dreams would create a secret journal with pawgull words that turned him in to not being a pawgull kid. But it did and my life as I knew it would never be the same.

From that day forward, I was never made fun of again and the nickname gidlader stuck with me, which eventually I came to like. My popularity soared after my birthday party and I became nook nooks with almost everyone at school, or at least they acknowledged my existence.

Even the skunkster and the no-gooders and I became somewhat friendly and my time of hiding out in the library was done. As for Grace, we quickly became great nook nooks and we were inseparable. We did everything together.

It was truly the greatest daydream I had ever dreamed up.

My days as a time dreamer were far from over. As the 6th grade continued, I still had my dreams of other worlds and I still brought things back, learning more and more about each place.

I never forgot about my promise to Grace about bringing her into a time dream with me. However, I still didn't understand it all and I was a bit skeptical on bringing her into one.

That didn't scare Grace at all. She still wanted to try it. She would ask me all the time if I had done any experiments that would make it possible for her to enter my time dreams. The truth was that I hadn't and so that was what I told her.

I initially started out wanting to make my promise to Grace my sole mission because I really didn't want to break my promise to her. But as the school year went on, I got so wrapped up with my newfound popularity and ruling the school that I completely pushed the Grace mission aside. School was fun and I was excited about going there every day. Kids liked me now and for the first time in my life I had nook nooks. It consumed me with happiness and I embraced every second of it. The only downfall of that was that it became all that I cared about.

It was during that time that I remembered about the wish-wish box. Three years had gone by since I had put my first wish into the box. I had waited anxiously, never giving up hope, that one day it would be time to open the box back up.

Well, that time had finally come.

Before I released my wish, I had to call my Aunt Lacy and tell her what had happened.

"Aunt Lacy, my wish, it finally came true!" I told her in excitement.

"I'm so happy for you, Dilby," she said. "See, wishes do come true after all."

"They sure do, Aunt Lacy," I said. "Thank you for giving me the wishwish box. This wouldn't have happened if it wasn't for you."

"Well, good things happen to good people, Dilby," she said. "You know what you have to do now, right?"

"I do," I replied confidently.

Later that night, before bed, I took the wishwish box from on top of my dresser, set it on the window sill, and opened my window. I removed the key from around my neck and inserted it into the lock of the box. I slowly turned the key to the right until the top popped open, releasing my wish out my bedroom window and out into the world.

My wish of becoming a cool kid had come true after all.

I still had many more wishes I wanted to come true so I decided to make another one. I thought up the wish I wanted, blew it into my fist, released it into the wishwish box, and closed it, locking it with key. I then put the key back around my neck where it would stay until the day I would take it off to open up the box again.

By the time 6th grade ended, I hadn't done one experiment to see if it was possible to bring Grace into my time dreams. I spent so much time focusing on myself that I completely ignored the promise I made to Grace. I felt terrible about it and I knew I had to make it right the only way I knew how.

It was time to put my social life on hold and get down to conducting my experiments. Failure was not an option and I was determined, no matter the consequences, to make Grace a time dreamer like me.

On the night of the last day of 6th grade, I laid in bed looking out at the smooneys, thinking about all that had happened that year. My life had truly changed in so many ways, but I had a feeling that this was only the beginning of what was to come.

As I thought about Grace and how I could test my time dreams, my eyes got heavy and my mind drifted away and I fell into a dream.

My eyes opened to a thick white blanket of fog. I couldn't see more than a few feet in front of me. The air was thin and it made it hard to breath.

I slowly stepped forward taking notice of the uneven terrain below my feet. Slowly the fog swept away and I could see that I was back on the rocky mountainside. Up ahead I saw the cave I once visited many years before and everything looked the same from what I could remember.

This was the first time I had dreamed of the same place twice and I wasn't sure why I had dreamed of going back there. Surely, there must be something special to that dream, but I didn't know what it was.

As I made my way to the opening, the cave once again began to speak as the air rushed out and blew my hair back. It had asked if I knew why I had returned. I replied that I didn't know, but it was clear that something wanted me there. It told me I had unfinished business and that the answers I was seeking was inside. All I had to do was enter its mouth.

I remembered the first time I was there and that I refused to go inside because I was scared. I often wondered what I had missed out on by not going inside. Would my life have been different than what it was? Would it have been better or worse? Either way, I was given another chance to enter the unknown and I wasn't about to make the same mistake twice.

I was stronger now and more confident with myself as the fear I once had was overcome with intrigue and desire.

I wanted to know what was inside. I needed to know what was inside.

The cave gave no answers when I asked what I would find. It simply said enter and you will see. The anticipation was building and it was time to seek out what it was I was brought there for.

The cave opened its mouth wider, making it big enough for me to walk into. I took a deep breath and cautiously made my way inside the dark abyss. After I fully entered inside the cave opening, it closed back up, returning to its original smaller opening.

I stood just inside not knowing what to do as I took in the surroundings. The air was still and had a stale scent to it. There was basically zero visibility in front of me and I could only see a few feet around me, which was lit up by the shallow light that squeezed its way inside from the cave opening.

I moved to one side of the cave and placed my hands on the jagged rock wall. The wall was rough and a little damp, giving off a slimy sensation. I began to slowly move ahead, using my hands to guide my way.

Aside from the noise of the shuffling of my feet, I heard a faint sound echoing from up ahead in the distance, like a muffled chant. The sound kept repeating over and over, getting louder and clearer with every blind step I took. My heart began to beat faster with anticipation, as well as a little fear.

Then, I saw a tiny speck of light growing larger as I made my way toward it. The closer I went to it, the brighter it got. It was almost blinding.

A loud noise suddenly erupted, like a deep base line. BMMMMMMMMMMM!

It was deafening as I dropped to my knees and put my hands over my ears, squeezing my eyes shut. The noise just kept reverberating louder within the cave walls as I could feel it beating in my chest. I couldn't take it anymore and I wanted it to stop.

And then it did.

I uncovered my ears and opened my eyes. The blinding light was gone and it was once again pitch black in front of me. As I stared into the darkness I began to see something moving toward me. It was starting to take shape as I quickly got to my feet and took a few steps back.

As it got closer and closer, the light from the opening had outlined the shape, resembling that of a person. When it stopped in front of me, I could see it was dressed in a hooded cloak, shielding its face from being seen.

Its presence was making me fearful as it stood there silent and menacing. I wasn't sure of what to do, but I knew I couldn't run away. I had to face whatever that thing was. I went into the cave looking for answers and understanding of why I had returned to the cave, and I wasn't going to leave until I found it.

"Who are you?" I asked with trepidation in my voice.

The figure raised its arms and removed the hood from its head. I was confused beyond belief as my mind tried to wrap itself around who it was that I was looking at.

"Aunt Lacy?" I said in complete shock and awe. "What are you…how are you here?"

"You didn't think you were the only time dreamer now, did you?" Aunt Lacy said.

"You're a time dreamer?" I said excitedly. "You mean that's actually a real thing?"

"It is and I am, just like you are, Dilby," Aunt Lacy said.

"Whoa! I just thought it was a cool name I made up to call myself." I said, still trying to process what was happening.

"You came here once before, 3 years ago, but you didn't come inside the cave," Aunt Lacy said. "Why did you never go in?"

"I was scared," I said.

"Not anymore, it seems," Aunt Lacy said. "You've grown."

"And changed," I said confidently.

She smiled and shook her head in acknowledgement.

"You remember the story of how you were born?" Aunt Lacy asked.

"You mean about the lighting storm?" I said.

"Yes. But that storm, it was no fluke like you were told, Dilby," Aunt Lacy said. "That storm was for you. You were chosen that night to be who you are."

"What do you mean?" I said.

"Your dreams, the worlds you travel to, bringing things back, those are all gifts," Aunt Lacy said.

"I don't understand." I said. "Gifts for what?"

Aunt Lacy extended her arm out to me.

"Come on, Dilby, let me show you," Aunt Lacy said. "You have a lot to learn."

I was totally blown away by all this and by what it all meant. But Aunt Lacy gave me reassurance and comfort as she always did. As odd as the whole thing was, I had no reason to be afraid.

"Where we going?" I asked, taking her hand with little hesitation.

"To show you what it means to be a time dreamer," Aunt Lacy said with a smile.

She turned and we walked hand in hand, disappearing into the darkness.

A SPECIAL PAGE TO WRITE YOUR OWN LIST OF WEIRD WORDS AND DEFINITIONS

ACKNOWLEDGMENTS

I first have to acknowledge my parents for the life they have given me. For all they have done, they could never know the depths of my gratitude and I could never say thank you enough. I love and miss you both.

Without an idea, there are no words. Without words, there is no book. This book started with an idea from just a few words that my girls, Morgan and Mallory, made up and told to me. It was words that they scribbled down on a piece of paper, conceived in their own little minds that had no meaning to me, but meant something to them. The more I looked at those words, the more excited I got about them. I've been wanting to write a children's book for a while and this was exactly the inspiration I was looking for to do so. Thank you my lovelies for showing me a glimpse into your imaginative minds and pushing me to go beyond my own limits. I would not be writing this if it weren't for you both.

Thanks to Lauren Doyle Davis for stepping in at the last minute with all your great notes and making sure I got my "commas" and "and's" in the right spots.

Thanks to John Fox for helping me to transform this book in the way in which it needed to be. Your editing notes and support were invaluable during this process.

Thanks to the creative team at Bookbaby for putting this all together.

Thanks to all my family and friends who have supported me and continue to support my work.

And special thanks to my amazing wife, Jen, who supported me and pushed me to get it done. Sorry for all the long days and nights I spent working to put words on the page. Your patience, encouragement, and support never went unnoticed. Thank you baby, I love you so much.

Lets do it again!

ABOUT THE AUTHOR

Tony J. Perri has worked for 15 years in the film and television industry and has written and directed an award winning independent feature film and a short film. He lives in Mesa, AZ with his wife and two daughters and his two dogs. *The Dilbonary* is his first children's book and will soon release a picture book. You can visit him online at www.verticalturtlepublishing.com